Charles Steigerwalt

Catalogue of a $12,000 Collection

Of Choice United States and Foreign Coins, Paper, Money, Medals, Etc. No. 26

Charles Steigerwalt

Catalogue of a $12,000 Collection
Of Choice United States and Foreign Coins, Paper, Money, Medals, Etc. No. 26

ISBN/EAN: 9783742832221

Manufactured in Europe, USA, Canada, Australia, Japa

Cover: Foto ©Andreas Hilbeck / pixelio.de

Manufactured and distributed by brebook publishing software
(www.brebook.com)

Charles Steigerwalt

Catalogue of a $12,000 Collection

$12,000 COLLECTION

OF

CHOICE UNITED STATES AND FOREIGN COINS, PAPER MONEY, MEDALS, ETC.

For Sale by CHAS. STEIGERWALT,

130 East King Street, Lancaster, Pa.

No. 26.　　　　ESTABLISHED 1878.　　　　SEPTEMBER, 1891.

REMARKS.

Please Read. Send orders early to prevent disappointment. Do not order anything you have not a reasonable expectation of buying if found correct, and return anything not desired as soon as possible after receipt of goods. Some of the coins, etc., in this list are out on approval now, but are included, as they may be returned. Coins sent on approval to responsible buyers. Remittances should be made by Money Order, Postal Note, Registered Letter, Check or Draft. Don't send stamps of high values. Address all letters plainly, and make money orders, etc., payable to Chas. Steigerwalt, 130 East King Street, Lancaster, Pa.

Note. This collection is particularly choice, and is the largest ever offered for sale at fixed prices. It contains many gems, and all the rarities in the U. S. silver and copper series, except the 1804 dollar. In addition will be found choice lines of paper money, foreign gold, silver and copper coins, ancient coins, medals, numismatic books, curios, etc. The prices have been made

United States Gold.

1795.   Eagle.   Uncirculated.   Proof surface.   25.00.

1797.   Eagle.   *Four stars facing.*   About uncirculated.   Semi-proof surface.   Extra rare.   75.00.

1797.   Eagle.   *Six stars facing.*   Uncirculated.   Brilliant mint bloom.   A beauty.   17.50.

1798.   Eagle.   *Four stars facing.*   Very fine and rare.   60.00.

1799.   Eagle.   Uncirculated.   Brilliant mint bloom.   A beauty.   15.00.

1800.   Eagle.   Uncirculated.   Brilliant mint bloom.   A beauty.   17.50.

1801.   Eagle.   Uncirculated.   Brilliant mint bloom.   A beauty.   17.50.

1803.   Eagle.   Barely circulated.   Mint bloom.   13.50.

1804.   Eagle.   Uncirculated.   Semi-proof.   50.00.

1795.   Half Eagle.   Close date.   *Proof.*   12.50.

1795.   Half Eagle.   Wide date.   *Proof.*   12.50.

1796 over '95.   Half Eagle.   Very fine.   25.00.

1798.   Half Eagle.   *Proof.*   10.00.

1800.   Half Eagle.   Uncirculated.   Brilliant mint bloom.   A beauty.   8.50.

1802 over '01.   Half Eagle.   Uncirculated.   Brilliant mint bloom.   A beauty.   8.50.

1803.   Half Eagle.   Uncirculated.   Proof surface.   A beauty.   8.50.

1804.   Half Eagle.   Uncirculated.   Brilliant mint bloom.   A beauty.   8.50.

1805.   Half Eagle.   Proof surface.   A beauty.   8.50.

1806.   Half Eagle.   Blunt 6.   Extremely fine.   Lustre.   6.50.

1806.   Half Eagle.   Pointed 6.   Uncirculated.   Proof surface.   7.50.

1807.   Half Eagle.   Head to right.   Uncirculated.   Mint bloom.   7.50.

1807. Half Eagle. Head to left. Uncirculated. Mint bloom. 7.50.
1808. Half Eagle. Uncirculated. Mint bloom. A beauty. 7.50.
1809. Half Eagle. Uncirculated. Mint bloom. A beauty. 7.50.
1810. Half Eagle. Large date. Uncirculated. Mint bloom. 7.00.
1810. Half Eagle. Small date. Uncirculated. Proof surface. 8.00.
1811. Half Eagle. Uncirculated. 7.00.
1812. Half Eagle. Uncirculated. 7.00.
1813. Half Eagle. Uncirculated. 7.00.
1823. Half Eagle. Uncirculated. Brilliant mint lustre. 20.00.
1826. Half Eagle. Uncirculated. Very rare. 25.00.
1834. Half Eagle. *Old type.* Uncirculated. Bold impression. Brilliant mint lustre. Semi-proof. 15.00.
1834. Half Eagle. *New type.* Proof. 6.50.
1863. Half Eagle. Brilliant proof. 7.50.
1796. Quarter Eagle. Without stars. Uncirculated. Mint bloom. 30.00.
1797. Quarter Eagle. Very fine. 50.00.
1798. Quarter Eagle. Uncirculated. Mint bloom. Proof surface. 20.00.
1802. Quarter Eagle. About a brilliant proof. 12.50.
1804. Quarter Eagle. Barely circulated. 8.50.
1805. Quarter Eagle. Barely circulated. Brilliant mint bloom. 8.50.
1806 over '04. Quarter Eagle. Centre not well struck up (all that way), otherwise sharp impression. Brilliant mint lustre, semi-proof surface. Extremely rare. 50.00.
1806 over '05. Quarter Eagle. Extra fine. Excessively rare. 50.00.
1807. Quarter Eagle. Very fine. 7.50.
1808. Quarter Eagle. Barely circulated. Brilliant mint bloom. 12.50.
1824. Quarter Eagle. Barely if any circulated. 17.50.
1825. Quarter Eagle. Uncirculated. Semi-proof. 20.00.
1827. Quarter Eagle. Uncirculated. Brilliant mint lustre. 20.00.
1829. Quarter Eagle. Uncirculated. Proof surface. 10.00.
1830. Quarter Eagle. Uncirculated. Semi-proof surface. 6.00.
1831. Quarter Eagle. *Brilliant proof.* 12.00.
1832. Quarter Eagle. Uncirculated. Brilliant mint bloom. 7.50.
1833. Quarter Eagle. Uncirculated. Brilliant mint bloom. 7.50.
1834. Quarter Eagle. *Brilliant proof.* 5.00.
1835. Quarter Eagle. Semi-proof. Handsome. 4.00.
1836. Quarter Eagle. Uncirculated. Brilliant mint bloom. 3.50.
1838. Quarter Eagle. Uncirculated. Brilliant mint bloom. 3.50.
1882. Quarter Eagle. Brilliant proof. 3.50.
1883. Quarter Eagle. Brilliant proof. 3.50.
1885. Quarter Eagle. Brilliant proof. 3.50.

1889.   Quarter Eagle.   Brilliant proof.   3.50.
1849.   Dollar.   Uncirculated.   Sharp little beauty.   2.50.
1850.   Dollar.   Uncirculated.   2.50.
1851.   Dollar.   Uncirculated.   Sharp little beauty.   2.50.
1852.   Dollar.   Uncirculated.   Sharp little beauty.   2.50.
1853.   Dollar.   Uncirculated.   Sharp little beauty.   2.50.
1854.   Dollar.   Small.   Uncirculated.   Sharp little beauty.   2.50.
1854.   Dollar.   Large.   Uncirculated.   2.00.
1855.   Dollar.   Brilliant proof.   12.50.
1855.   Dollar.   Uncirculated.   2.00.
1856.   Dollar.   Brilliant proof.   12.50.
1856.   Dollar.   Small date.   Straight 5.   Uncirculated.   5.00.
1856.   Dollar.   Large date.   Slanting 5.   Uncirculated.   3.50.
1857.   Dollar.   Uncirculated.   2.00.
1858.   Dollar.   Brilliant proof.   10.00.
1858.   Dollar.   Uncirculated.   2.00.
1859.   Dollar.   Uncirculated.   2.00.
1860.   Dollar.   Brilliant proof.   5.00.
1860.   Dollar.   Uncirculated.   2.50.
1861.   Dollar.   Brilliant proof.   5.00.
1861.   Dollar.   Uncirculated.   2.50.
1862.   Dollar.   Uncirculated.   2.00.
1864.   Dollar.   Uncirculated.   Brilliant mint bloom.   17.50.
1865.   Dollar.   Uncirculated.   Semi-proof.   10.00.
1866.   Dollar.   Uncirculated.   Semi-proof.   7.50.
1867.   Dollar.   Uncirculated.   Semi-proof.   5.00.
1868.   Dollar.   Brilliant proof.   5.00.
1869.   Dollar.   Uncirculated.   Brilliant mint bloom.   3.50.
1871.   Dollar.   Uncirculated.   Brilliant mint bloom.   3.50.
1872.   Dollar.   *Proof.*   5.00.
1873.   Dollar.   Uncirculated.   Brilliant.   2.00.
1874.   Dollar.   Uncirculated.   Brilliant.   2.00.
1875.   Dollar.   Brilliant proof.   20.00.
1876.   Dollar.   *Brilliant proof.*   7.50.
1877.   Dollar.   *Proof.*   4.00.
1880.   Dollar.   Brilliant proof.   2.50.
1881.   Dollar.   Brilliant proof.   2.50.
1882.   Dollar.   Semi-proof.   2.00.
1883.   Dollar.   Brilliant proof.   2.50.
1884.   Dollar.   Brilliant proof.   2.50.
1885.   Dollar.   Brilliant proof.   2.50.
1886.   Dollar.   Brilliant proof.   2.50.
1887.   Dollar.   Brilliant proof.   2.50.
1888.   Dollar.   Brilliant proof.   2.50.
1889.   Dollar.   Brilliant proof.   2.50.
1849.   Dollar.   O. Mint.   Barely circulated.   2.00.
1849.   Dollar.   D. Mint.   Very fine.   3.00.
1849.   Dollar.   C. Mint.   Barely circulated.   3.00.

1850. Dollar. O. Mint. Very fine. 3.00.
1850. Dollar. D. Mint. Fine. 3.50.
1851. Dollar. O. Mint. Barely circulated. 2.00.
1851. Dollar. C. Mint. Extremely fine. 3.00.
1851. Dollar. D. Mint. Barely circulated. 3.50.
1852. Dollar. O. Mint. Extremely fine. 2.00.
1853. Dollar. C. Mint. Very fine. 3.00.
1855. Dollar. O. Mint. Extremely fine. 2.50.
1856. Dollar. S. Mint. *Small head of 1855.* Extremely fine. 3.50.
1857. Dollar. S. Mint. Fine. 3.50.
1857. Dollar. C. Mint. Very good. 3.00.
1859. Dollar. C. Mint. Very fine. 3.00.
1859. Dollar. D. Mint. Extremely fine. 3.50.
1859. Dollar. S. Mint. Extremely fine. 3.50.
1860. Dollar. S. Mint. Very fine, but pierced. 2.00.
Georgia. "C. Bechtler at Rutherford, 5 Dollars." Rev.,
    "Georgia Gold. 128 G. 22 carats." Semi-proof.
    10.00.
Carolina. "A. Bechtler, Rutherford." 5 Dollars. Fine. 7.00.
Carolina. "A. Bechtler." Dollar. About uncirculated. 2.00.
Carolina. "Ruthford. Bechtler." Dollar. Fine. 1.75.

Set of United States Three Dollars.

1854 to 1888. Full set of Three Dollars except 1875 and 1889.
The 1858, 1861, 1869, 1873 and 1874 are barely touched; the others
are either mint bloom or proof. The 1876, 1877, 1880 to 1884,
1886 to 1888 are all brilliant proofs, some of the others semi-proof.
A nice set. 34 pcs. 150.00.

United States Proof Sets.

1846. Proof Set. Contains Dollar, Half Dollar, Quarter, Dime,
    Half Dime, and two Copper Cents (the tall 6 and the
    "Dutch 6." Half Cent lacking. The "Dutch 6" cent is
    sharp and perfect, but not as brilliant as proofs of later
    years, but the rest of the set is in nice condition. The
    Dime and Half Dime are beauties, and very rare in this
    condition. 90.00.
1857. Proof Set. Similar to last. 50.00.
1858. Proof Set. 7 pcs. 65.00.
1859. Proof Set. 7 pcs. 6.00.
1860. Proof Set. 7 pcs. 6.00.
1861. Proof Set. 7 pcs. 6.00.
1862. Proof Set. 7 pcs. 6.00.
1863. Proof Set. 7 pcs. 6.00.
1864. Proof Set. 9 pcs. 10.00.
1865. Proof Set. 9 pcs. 8.00.
1866. Proof Set. 10 pcs. 6.00.
1867. Proof Set. 10 pcs. 6.00.

1868. Proof Set. 10 pcs. 6.00.
1869. Proof Set. 10 pcs. 5.00.
1870. Proof Set. 10 pcs. 5.00.
1871. Proof Set. 10 pcs. 5.00.
1872. Proof Set. 10 pcs. 5.00.
1873. Proof Set. Old Style. 10 pcs. 6.50.
1873. Proof Set. Trade. 7 pcs. 5.00.
1874. Proof Set. 7 pcs. 5.00.
1875. Proof Set. 8 pcs. 5.00.
1876. Proof Set. 8 pcs. 5.00.
1877. Proof Set. 8 pcs. 9.00.
1878. Proof Set. Includes both dollars and the rare 20 cent. 6.00.
1879. Proof Set. Both dollars. 4.00.
1880. Proof Set. Both dollars. 4.00.
1881. Proof Set. Both dollars. 4.50.
1882. Proof Set. Both dollars. 4.50.
1883. Proof Set. Both dollars. 4.50.
1884. Proof Set. 4.00.
1885. Proof Set. 4.00.
1886. Proof Set. 4.00.
1887. Proof Set. 4.00.
1888. Proof Set. 4.00.
1889. Proof Set. 4.00.
1890. Proof Set. 3.50.
1891. Proof Set. 3.50.

United States Dollars.

1794. Very fine. An unusually even impression: stars, head and date well struck, as is also the reverse. 125.00.
1795. Flowing hair. Very handsome specimen with semi-proof surface. Uncirculated. A gem. 35.00.
1795. Flowing hair. A beautiful specimen. Barely touched. Mint lustre. 15.00.
1795. Fillet head. Uncirculated. Proof surface. 75.00.

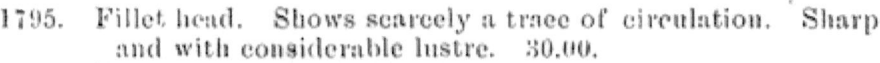

1795. Fillet head. Shows scarcely a trace of circulation. Sharp and with considerable lustre. 30.00.

1795. Fillet head. Almost equal to last. 20.00.

1796. Large date. Quite fine. 5.00.

1796. Small date. Very fine. 7.50.

1797. Seven stars facing. Very fine. 7.50.

1797. Six stars facing. Uncirculated. Brilliant mint lustre. 35.00.

1797. Six stars facing. Very fine. 7.50.

1798. Fifteen stars. *Small eagle*. Fine. 10.00.

1798. Thirteen stars. *Small eagle*. Very fine. 7.50.

1798. Large eagle. But little circulated. Some lustre. 3.00.

1799. *Five stars facing*. Fine. 5.00.

1799 over '98. But little worn. 3.00.

1799. Strictly uncirculated. Brilliant mint bloom. 5.00.

1800. Barest touch of circulation. Brilliant mint bloom. 8.50.

1801. Very fine. Considerable lustre. 7.50.

1802. Uncirculated. Brilliant mint bloom. 25.00.

1802. Barely touched on most prominent parts. Mint bloom. 10.00.

1802 over '01. Barely touched on most prominent parts. Mint lustre. 10.00.

1803. Large 3. Could be called uncirculated. Sharp, handsome, with semi-proof surface. A beauty. 15.00.

1803. Small 3. Very trifling circulation. Sharp and with some proof surface. Scarce variety. 10.00.

1836. Brilliant proof. Sharp and handsome. 15.00.

1836. *Gobrecht in field*. Brilliant proof. 65.00. About uncirculated. Extremely rare. 40.00.

1838. *Brilliant proof*. 85.00.

1839. *Brilliant proof*. 60.00.

1840. *Brilliant proof*. 15.00.

1840. Uncirculated. Proof surface. 3.50.

1841. Uncirculated. Mint bloom. Semi-proof. 3.00.

1842. Uncirculated. Mint bloom. 2.00.

1843.   Uncirculated.   Mint bloom.   2.00.
1844.   *Brilliant proof.* 20.00.
1844.   Uncirculated.   Mint bloom.   3.50.
1845.   *Brilliant proof.*   A few light haymarks.   15.00.
1845.   Barely circulated.   Mint bloom.   2.50.
1846.   Uncirculated.   Mint bloom.   2.50.
1846.   O. Mint.   Barely touched.   Mint bloom.   Semi-proof surface.   3.50.
1847.   Uncirculated.   Mint bloom.   Semi-proof.   Handsome specimen.   3.00.
1848.   Uncirculated.   Mint bloom.   3.50.
1849.   Uncirculated.   Proof surface.   3.00.
1850.   *Brilliant proof.*   25.00.
1851.   *Brilliant proof.*   65.00.
1852.   Uncirculated.   Brilliant mint lustre.   60.00.
1853.   Uncirculated.   Brilliant mint lustre.   5.00.
1854.   *Brilliant proof.*   30 00.
1855.   *Brilliant proof.*   25.00.
1856.   Uncirculated.   Brilliant mint bloom.   Scarcely perceptible pin scratch in field.   3.50.
1857.   *Proof.*   A few stars not sharp.   6.00.
1858.   *Brilliant proof.*   60.00.
1859.   O. Mint.   Uncirculated.   Brilliant mint lustre.   2.50.
1859.   S. Mint.   Barely circulated.   Very rare.   7.50.
1860.   O. Mint.   Uncirculated.   Brilliant mint lustre.   3.00.
1865.   Dollar, half and quarter.   With legend " In God we Trust " above eagle on reverse.   Brilliant proofs.   Excessively rare.   Set for 75.00.

United States Half Dollars.

1794.   Barely circulated.   Considerable lustre.   One of the best of the date I have seen.   35.00.
1794.   Very fine.   Bold impression.   Date strong.   8.00.
1795.   Uncirculated.   Mint lustre.   Planchet file marks.   10.00.
1796.   Sixteen stars.   Very good and bold.   75.00.
1796.   Fifteen stars.   Fine for date, but seven minute pin-nicks on head.   60.00.
1797.   Very fine specimen of this rare date.   125.00.

1801. Extremely fine. Choice specimen. 15.00.
1802. Extremely fine. 15.00.
1805 over '04. Very fine. 7.50.
1806. *Proof.* 10.00.
1806. No stem in eagle's claw. Uncirculated. Brilliant mint bloom. 10.00.
1807. Head to right. Uncirculated. Brilliant mint bloom. 10.00.
1807. Head to left. About uncirculated. Sharp. 3.50.
1808 over '07. Barely touched. Mint lustre. 3.00.
1808. Perfect date. Uncirculated. Brilliant mint lustre. 4.00.
1809. Uncirculated. Brilliant mint bloom. Very sharp and handsome. 3.00.
1810. Uncirculated. Brilliant mint lustre. 3.00.
1811. Uncirculated. Brilliant mint lustre. 2.00.
1811. Period in date. Brilliant mint lustre. 3.00.
1812. Uncirculated. Brilliant mint lustre. Sharp and handsome. 2.00.
1813. Uncirculated. Brilliant mint lustre. Sharp. 2.00.
1814. Uncirculated. Brilliant mint lustre. 2.00.
1815. Uncirculated. Semi-proof. One of the handsomest specimens of this date known. 25.00.
1815. Uncirculated. Sharp. 15.00.
1817. Uncirculated. Mint bloom. 2.00.
1818. *Brilliant proof.* 15.00.
1818 over '17. Uncirculated. Mint bloom. Sharp and handsome. 2.50.
1819. Uncirculated. Mint lustre. 1.00.
1820. Small date. Uncirculated. Mint bloom. 2.00.
1820. Large date. Curled 2. Uncirculated. Brilliant mint lustre. 2.50.
1820. Large, wide date. Knobbed 2. Uncirculated. Brilliant mint bloom. Sharp and handsome. 3.00.
1820. Over '19. *Proof.* A beauty. 10.00.
1821. Uncirculated. Mint lustre. Sharp and handsome. 2.00.
1822. Uncirculated. Mint lustre. Sharp and handsome. 2.00.
1823. Uncirculated. Mint bloom. 1.50.
1824. Uncirculated. Mint lustre. Handsome. 1.50.
1824. Double profile. Uncirculated. Mint lustre. 1.50.
1825. Uncirculated. Mint lustre. Handsome. 1.50.
1826. Uncirculated. Proof impression. 3.50.
1827. *Proof.* 5.00.
1828. Plain 2. Small date. Uncirculated. Mint bloom. Handsome. 1.50.
1828. Curled 2. *Proof.* 7.50.
1829. *Proof.* Splendid specimen. 7.50.
1829 over '21. Uncirculated. Mint lustre. 1.50.
1830. *Brilliant proof.* 12.50.
1831. Uncirculated. Mint lustre. 1.00.

1832. Uncirculated. Mint lustre. 1.00.
1833. Uncirculated. Mint lustre. 1.00.
1834. Large date. *Brilliant proof.* 12.50.
1834. Small date. Uncirculated. Mint lustre. 1.00.
1835. Uncirculated. Mint lustre. 1.00.
1836. Uncirculated. Brilliant mint lustre. Sharp and handsome. 2.00.
1836' Milled edge. Brilliant proof, a little haymarked. 15.00.
1837' Uncirculated. Handsome mint bloom. 2.00.
1838' Uncirculated. Mint lustre. 1.00.
1839' Head. Uncirculated. Mint lustre. 1.00.
1839' O. Mint. (O under head). Uncirculated. Brilliant mint lustre. 2.50.
1839. Liberty seated. *Without drapery from elbow to knee.* Uncirculated. 2.50.
1839. Liberty seated. *With drapery from elbow to knee.* Uncirculated. Handsome. 2.50.
1840. Uncirculated. Mint lustre. Very handsome specimen. 2.50.
1840. O. Mint. Large O. Uncirculated. Brilliant mint bloom. 2.50.
1840. O. Mint. Small O. Uncirculated. Brilliant mint bloom. 2.50.
1841. O. Mint. Uncirculated. Mint lustre. 1.50.
1842. Large date. Proof surface. Very handsome specimen. 3.00.
1842. Small date. Uncirculated. Proof surface. 2.50.
1842. Large date. O. Mint. Uncirculated. Brilliant mint lustre. 2.00.
1843. Uncirculated. Sharp. Proof surface. 2.00.
1843. O. Mint. Uncirculated. Mint lustre. 2.00.
1844. *Proof.* 4.00.
1844. O. Mint. Uncirculated. Mint lustre. Semi-proof. 3.00.
1845. O. Mint. Uncirculated. Semi-proof. 1.50.
1846. Uncirculated. Mint lustre. 1.00.
1846. O. Mint. Uncirculated. Mint lustre. 2.00.
1847. Uncirculated. Mint lustre. Beautiful sharp specimen. 2.00.
1847. O. Mint. Uncirculated. Mint lustre. Slight proof surface. 2.50.
1848. Uncirculated. Mint lustre. 1.50.
1848. O. Mint. Uncirculated. Mint lustre. Sharp. 2.50.
1849. *Brilliant proof.* 7.50.
1849. O. Mint. Uncirculated. Mint lustre. 2.00.
1850. Uncirculated. Mint lustre. Very sharp and handsome. 2.00.
1850. O. Mint. Uncirculated. Mint lustre. Handsome. 2.00.
1851. O. Mint. Uncirculated. Mint lustre. 2.50.
1851. P. Mint. Uncirculated. Mint lustre. 2.50.
1852. P. Mint. Uncirculated. Mint lustre. 6.00.
1852. O. Mint. *Proof impression.* 7.50.

1853.   Uncirculated.   Mint lustre.   A beauty.   2.00.
1854.   *Brilliant proof.*   7.50.
1854.   O. Mint.   Uncirculated.   Mint lustre.   Semi-proof.   2.00.
1855.   O. Mint.   Uncirculated.   Mint lustre.   1.50.
1856.   O. Mint.   Uncirculated.   Mint lustre.   1.50.
1858.   Uncirculated.   Mint lustre.   Handsome, sharp specimen.
    1.25.

United States Quarters.

1796.   *Sharp proof.*   Beautiful specimen.   75.00.
1796.   Extremely fine, barely circulated.   20.00.
1804.   Quite fine.   Unusually bold.   15.00.
1805.   Very fine and bold.   3.00.
1806   The centre of obverse and corresponding portion of reverse
    a little weak from weak die, otherwise uncirculated, bril-
    liant mint lustre.   7.50.
1806 over '05.   Fine and bold.   1.50.
1807.   But little circulated.   Considerable lustre.   10.00.
1807.   Fine and bold.   2.00.
1815.   Small E above head.   Uncirculated.   Mint lustre.   3.00.
1818.   Uncirculated.   Mint lustre.   2.00.
1819.   Barely circulated.   Mint lustre.   2.00.
1820.   Large O.   *Proof.*   10.00.
1820.   Small O.   Semi-proof.   Rare.   15.00.
1821.   *Brilliant proof.*   7.50.
1821.   Uncirculated.   Mint lustre.   3.00.
1822.   Uncirculated.   Mint lustre.   Handsome.   8.50.
1823.   In good condition for this rare date, the date bold.   60.00.
1824.   Quite fine.   Rare so choice.   5.00.
1825.   Uncirculated.   Mint lustre.   3.00.
1827.   *Brilliant proof.*   150.00.
1828.   *Proof.*   7.50.
1828.   Uncirculated.   Mint lustre.   Slight nick on neck.   1.50.
1831.   Uncirculated.   Mint lustre.   1.00.
1832.   Uncirculated.   Mint lustre.   2.00.
1834.   Uncirculated.   Mint lustre.   1.00.
1835.   Uncirculated.   Mint lustre.   1.00.
1836.   Uncirculated.   Mint lustre.   1.50.
1837.   *Proof.*   2.50.

1837.   Uncirculated.   Mint lustre.   1.00.
1842.   O. Mint.   Uncirculated.   Mint lustre.   1.50.
1843.   Uncirculated.   Mint lustre.   1.25.
1844.   O. Mint.   About uncirculated.   1.00.
1845.   Uncirculated.   Mint lustre.   A beauty.   1.50.
1846.   *Brilliant proof.*   10.00.
1847.   Uncirculated.   Mint lustre.   1.50.
1849.   *Brilliant proof.*   10.00.
1850.   Uncirculated.   Semi-proof.   1.50.
1852.   Uncirculated.   Mint lustre.   2.00.
1853.   *Proof.*   2.50.
1853.   *Without arrows or rays.*   Uncirculated.   Mint lustre.   15.00.
1856.   *Brilliant proof.*   10.00.
1857.   O. Mint.   Uncirculated.   Semi proof.   Handsome.   2.00.
1858.   Brilliant proof.   2.00.

United States Twenty Cents.

1875.   Brilliant proof.   1.00.
1876.   Brilliant proof.   1.00.
1876.   Uncirculated.   Brilliant mint lustre.   .50.
1877.   Brilliant proof.   3.00.
1878.   Brilliant proof.   2.50.

United States Dimes.

1796.   Cracked die.   Uncirculated.   Brilliant.   15.00.
1796.   Perfect die.   Uncirculated.   Brilliant mint lustre.   Very sharp and handsome.   20.00.
1797.   Thirteen stars.   The hair lines but little worn.   Extremely fine and best offered for some time.   25.00.
1797.   Sixteen stars.   Very fine, but centre of reverse scratched   12.50.
1798 over '97.   15 stars above eagle's head on reverse.   Very fine.   15.00.
1798 over '97.   13 stars above eagle's head on reverse.   Very good.   Very rare variety.   10.00.
1798.   Perfect date.   Except the stars to left, which are a little worn, the piece is almost uncirculated.   Nice specimen.   25.00.
1800.   Could almost be called uncirculated.   A beauty.   40.00.
1801.   Uncirculated.   Brilliant mint bloom.   75.00.
1801.   Barely touched by circulation.   But for the fact that a pin.

scratch extends from top of hair to bottom of bust, would be one of the finest known. 12.50.

1802. Very good for date. 6.00.
1803. Extremely fine. In this condition exceedingly rare. 25.00.
1804. Barely touched by circulation. The hair lines bold and sharp. Excelled by few. 75.00.
1804. Quite fine and bold, nearly all the hair lines show. 35.00.
1805. Uncirculated. Brilliant mint lustre. 15.00.
1807. Barely touched. Brilliant mint lustre. 3 light scratches. 5.00.
1807. Beard variety. Barest touch of circulation, hair lines sharp. 7.50.
1809. Uncirculated. Brilliant mint lustre. 50.00.
1809. Quite fine and bold. 5.00.
1811. Quite fine and bold. 5.00.
1811. Over '09. Scarcely touched by circulation. A handsome piece. 20.00.
1814. *Large date.* Uncirculated. Brilliant mint lustre. 7.50.
1820. Uncirculated. Large C in 10 C. Mint lustre. 5.00.
1821. *Large date.* Uncirculated. Mint lustre. 3.00.
1822. But little worn. Mint lustre. 15.00.
1823. Uncirculated. Mint lustre. 12.50.
1824. Quite fine. Much better than usually found. 2.00.
1825. *Brilliant proof. Sharp and perfect.* 20.00.
1825. Uncirculated. Brilliant mint bloom. 5.00.
1827. Uncirculated. Brilliant mint bloom. 5.00.
1828. Large date. But little worn. Considerable lustre. 2.00.
1828. *Small date.* Uncirculated. Sharp. Brilliant mint lustre. Handsome specimen. 7.50.
1829. Uncirculated. Brilliant mint lustre. Very sharp and handsome. 2.50.
1830. *Brilliant proof.* 10.00.
1830. Uncirculated. Brilliant mint bloom. Handsome. 2.00.
1831. *Brilliant proof.* 10.00.
1832. *Proof.* Nick on edge. 2.00.
1833. Uncirculated. Mint lustre. 1.50.
1834. *Brilliant proof.* 10.00.
1835. *Brilliant proof.* 10.00.
1835. Uncirculated. Brilliant mint bloom. Handsome. 2.00.
1836. Uncirculated. Mint lustre. 1.00.
1837. Head. Uncirculated. Mint lustre. 1.50.
1837. Liberty seated. Large date. Sharp brilliant proof. 12.50.
1837. Liberty seated. Small date. About uncirculated. Lustre. Rare. 1.50.
1838. *Without stars.* Uncirculated. Mint lustre. 10.00.
1838. *With stars.* Uncirculated. A beauty. Mint lustre. 1.50.
1839. Uncirculated. Brilliant mint lustre. Sharp. 2.00.
1840. Without drapery. *Brilliant proof.* 5.00.
1840. With drapery. Uncirculated. Mint bloom. 1.50.

1841.   Uncirculated.   Mint lustre.   1.25.
1841.   O. Mint.   Uncirculated.   Mint lustre.   1.50.
1842.   Uncirculated.   Mint lustre.   Slight proof surface.   3.50.
1843.   Uncirculated   Mint lustre.   1.25.
1845.   Uncirculated.   Mint lustre.   1.25.
1846.   Uncirculated.   10.00.
1848.   Uncirculated.   Mint lustre.   3.00.
1849.   *Brilliant proof.*   10.00.
1850.   Uncirculated.   Mint lustre.   1.25.
1851.   Uncirculated.   Mint lustre.   1.25.
1852.   *Brilliant proof.*   7.50.
1852.   Uncirculated.   Mint lustre.   1.00.
1853.   *Without arrows.*   Uncirculated.   Mint lustre.   1.50.
1853.   *With arrows.*   *Proof.*   2.50.
1853.   *With arrows.*   Uncirculated.   Mint lustre.   .75.
1854.   O. Mint.   Uncirculated.   .75.
1855   *Brilliant proof.*   7.50.
1855.   Uncirculated.   Mint lustre.   .50.
1856.   *Large date.*   Uncirculated.   Mint lustre.   1.50.
1856.   *Small date.*   Uncirculated.   Mint lustre.   1.25.
1856.   *Small date.*   O. Mint.   Uncirculated. Mint lustre.   Slight proof surface.   1.50.
1857.   Uncirculated.   Mint lustre.   .50.
1857.   O. Mint.   Uncirculated.   Mint lustre.   1.00.
1858.   *Brilliant proof.*   2.00.
1858.   Uncirculated. Mint lustre. Sharp, handsome specimen. .75.
1859.   O. Mint.   Uncirculated.   Mint lustre.   1.00.
1860.   S. Mint.   Uncirculated, brilliant mint lustre.   Extremely rare in this condition.   15.00.

United States Half Dimes.

1794.   Uncirculated with proof surface.   A gem.   25.00.
1795.   Uncirculated.   Semi-proof.   12.50.
1796.   Uncirculated.   Brilliant mint lustre.   Sharp impression. 35.00.
1796.   Barely touched by circulation.   Sharp and handsome. 20.00.
1797.   *Thirteen stars.*   Nick to left of date otherwise quite fine and bold.   3.50.
1797.   *Fifteen stars.*   Extremely fine.   Sharp and handsome. 15.00.

1797. *Sixteen stars.* Uncirculated. Brilliant mint lustre. Sharp and handsome. 30.00.
1800. Very fine. 3.50.
1800. LIBEKTY. Very good and bold. 2.00.
1801. Shows but little circulation. One of the best of this date. 20.00.
1802. A good specimen of this extremely rare date. 100.00.
1803. Large 8. Quite fine. Nearly all the hair lines show. 10.00.
1803. Small 8. Extremely fine. Scarce variety. 15.00.
1805. Barest touch of circulation. Sharp and handsome. 35.00.
1829. Uncirculated. Mint lustre. .50.
1830. Uncirculated. Mint lustre. .50.
1831. *Brilliant proof.* 7.50.
1831. Uncirculated. .75.
1832. Uncirculated. Semi-proof. .75.
1832. Knobbed 8. Uncirculated. Mint lustre. .75.
1833. Uncirculated. Mint lustre. .75.
1834. *Brilliant proof.* 10.00.
1834. Uncirculated. Mint lustre. .75.
1835. Large date. Uncirculated. Mint lustre. .75.
1835. Small date. Brilliant proof. 7.50.
1835. Small date. Uncirculated. Mint lustre. .50.
1836. Uncirculated. Mint lustre. .75.
1837. *Head.* Uncirculated. Mint lustre. .75.
1837. *No stars. Curved date. Brilliant proof.* 7.50.
1837. *No stars. Curved date.* Uncirculated. Mint bloom. Sharp. Beautiful specimen. 2.50.
1837. *No stars. Straight date.* Uncirculated. Mint bloom. 1.50.
1838. *No stars.* Uncirculated. Brilliant mint bloom. Extremely rare in this condition. 15.00.
1838. *With stars. Brilliant proof.* 7.50.
1838. *With stars.* Uncirculated. Mint lustre. 1.00.
1839. *Proof.* 2.50.
1840. *With drapery. Fine proof.* 5.00.
1840. *Without drapery.* Uncirculated. Mint lustre. Semi-proof. 1.50.
1841. *Brilliant proof.* 10.00.
1841. Uncirculated. Mint lustre. 1.25.
1842. *Brilliant proof.* 12.50.
1842. Uncirculated. Mint lustre. Sharp. Slight proof surface. 3.50.
1843. Uncirculated. Mint lustre. 1.00.
1844. P. Mint. *Brilliant proof.* 10.00.
1844. P. Mint. Uncirculated. Mint lustre. Some proof surface. A beauty. 3.50.
1845. Uncirculated. Semi-proof. 2.00.
1846. Uncirculated. Mint bloom. 15.00.
1847. *Brilliant proof.* 12.50.

1847. Uncirculated. Mint lustre. 1.00.
1848. Large date. Uncirculated. Brilliant mint bloom. 12.50.
1848. *Large date.* Very fine. Rare so choice. 5.00.
1848. *Small date.* Obverse brilliant proof; rev., mint bloom. A beauty. 10.00.
1849. *Brilliant proof.* 10.00.
1849. Uncirculated. Mint lustre. Some proof surface. 1.50.
1850. Uncirculated. Mint lustre. Sharp and handsome. 1.00.
1851. Uncirculated. Proof surface. 1.00.
1851. O. Mint. Uncirculated. Mint lustre. 1.00.
1852. Uncirculated. Mint lustre. .50.
1852. *Brilliant proof.* 7.50.
1853. *Without arrows.* Almost a brilliant proof. Handsome. 3.00.
1853. *With arrows.* Proof surface. 1.00.
1854. *Brilliant proof.* 7.50.
1854. Uncirculated. Mint lustre. .50.
1855. *Brilliant proof.* 7.50.
1855. Uncirculated. Mint lustre. .50.
1855. O. Mint. Uncirculated. Mint lustre. .50.
1856. *Brilliant proof.* 5.00.
1857. Uncirculated. Mint bloom. .50.
1857. O. Mint. *Brilliant proof.* 7.50.
1857. O. Mint. Uncirculated. Mint lustre. 1.00.
1858. *Brilliant proof.* 2.00.
1859. O. Mint. Uncirculated. Mint lustre. .50.
1860. *With stars. Proof.* 7.50.
1860. O. Mint. Uncirculated. Mint lustre. .75.

United States Silver Three Cents.

1851. Uncirculated. Mint lustre. Proof surface. 2.00.
1851. Uncirculated. Mint lustre. .50.
1851. O. Mint. Uncirculated. Mint lustre. .75.
1852. Uncirculated. Mint lustre. .50.
1853. Uncirculated. Mint lustre. .35.
1854. *Brilliant proof.* 7.50.
1854. Uncirculated. Mint lustre. 1.50.
1855. *Brilliant proof.* 7.50.
1855. Uncirculated. Mint lustre. 2.00.
1856. Uncirculated. Mint lustre. 1.50.
1857. Uncirculated. Mint lustre. .50.
1858. Brilliant proof. 2.00.
1858. Uncirculated. Mint lustre. .50.
1859. Brilliant proof. .75.
1860. Brilliant proof. .75.
1861. Brilliant proof. .75.
1862. Brilliant proof. .50.
1863. Uncirculated. Mint bloom. Rarer than proof. 1.00.
1864. Uncirculated. Mint bloom. Rarer than proof. 2.00.

1865. Uncirculated. Mint bloom. Rarer than proof. 1.50.
1866. Brilliant proof. 1.00.
1867. Brilliant proof. 1.00.
1868. Brilliant proof. 1.00.
1869. Brilliant proof. 1.50.
1870. Dull proof. .75.
1871. Uncirculated. Mint lustre. Semi-proof. 75.
1872. Brilliant proof. .75.
1873. Brilliant proof. 1.00.

United States Minor Coinage.

1856. Nickel Cent. Brilliant proof. 6.00.
1858. Nickel Cents. Large and small letters in legends. Brilliant
    proofs. Pair 2.00.
1859. Nickel Cent. Brilliant proof. .50.
1860. Nickel Cent. Brilliant proof. .75.
1861. Nickel Cent. Brilliant proof. 1.00.
1862. Nickel Cent. Brilliant proof. .40.
1863. Nickel Cent. Brilliant proof. .40.
1864. Nickel Cent. Brilliant proof. .75.
1865. Bronze Cent. Brilliant proof. .50.
1869. Two Cents. Brilliant proof. .50.
1866. Five Cents. *With rays.* Brilliant proof. .50.
1866. Five Cents. *Without rays. Brilliant proof.* Extremely
    rare. 5.00.
1867. Five Cents. *With rays. Brilliant proof.* Rare. 3.50.
1877. Five Cents. Brilliant proof. 2.00.
1873. Minor proof set. 1, 2, 3, 5 cents. 1.75.
1877. Minor proof set. 1, 3, 5 cents. 4.00.
1878. Minor proof set. 1, 3, 5 cents. .75.

United States Cents.

1793. Chain "Ameri." Extremely fine. Bold, clean reverse. Olive.
    50.00.
1793. Chain "America." No periods after " Liberty " and date.
    The masses of hair slightly worn, otherwise about un-
    circulated. Light olive. 50.00.
1793. Chain "America." Periods after "Liberty" and date.
    Nearly uncirculated. Brown. 25.00.
1793. Wreath. Broad head and leaves. Small date. Very fine
    specimen. 12.50.

1793. Wreath. Stem of leaves over 7 and 9 of date. Very fine. Light color. 15.00.

1793. Wreath. Stem above 9 of date. Lettered edge. Fine. Light brown. 10.00.

1793. Wreath. Stem above 9 of date. Vine and bars on edge (not often found on this variety). Very fine. Light brown with traces of original red. 15.00.

1793. Liberty Cap. Very good. Beaded milling complete on both sides. Steel color. 12.50.

1794. Maris No. 1. "1793 Head." The edge of obverse shows trifling bruises, but the cent is one of the best of this rare variety I have seen. Quite fine and of light olive color. 7.50.

1794. Maris No. 3. "Sans Milling." Fine. Brown. 2.00.

1794. Maris No. 5. "Young Head." Fine. Brown. 2.00.

1794. Maris No. 11. "Many Haired." Nearly fine. Brown. 1.50.

1794. Maris No. 12. "Scarred Head." Extremely fine. Light olive. 12.50.

1794. Maris No. 13. "Standless 4." Very fine. Brown. 3.50.

1794. Maris No. 14. "Abrupt Hair." Only touched on the masses of hair. Light olive. 12.50.

1794. Maris No. 20. "Fallen 4." Very fine. Brown. 4.00.

1794. Maris No. 21. "Short Bust." Very fine. Chocolate. 3.50.

1794. Maris No. 25. "The Ornate." Very fine. Steel color. 3.50.

1794. Maris No. 26. "Amiable Face." Very fine. Light brown. 3.50.

1794. Maris No. 28. "Large Planchet." Quite fine and bold. 2.00.

1794. Maris No. 29. "Marred Field." Fine. Light olive. 2.50.

1794. Maris No. 32. "Shielded Hair." About fine. Brown. 2.00.

1794. Maris No. 36. "The Plicæ." Nearly fine. Brown. 2.00.

1794. Maris No. 38. "Roman Plicæ." Fine. Light brown. 2.50.

1794. Maris No. 39. "1795 Head." Quite fine. Dark olive. 3.50.

1794. Maris No. 40. "Many Haired." Fine. Light brown. 2.50.

1794. Maris No. 42. "Trephined Head." About fine. 2.00.

1794. Maris No. 46. Very fine. Hair but little worn. 5.00.

1794. Maris No. 50. Fine. 3.00.

1795. Lettered Edge. Fractional mark regular. One berry on each side of ribbon bow. Uncirculated. Light olive. $5.00.

1795. Lettered Edge. Fractional mark irregular. Berry on left of ribbon bow, none on right. Extremely fine. Brown. 20.00.

1795. Thick planchet, but unlettered edge. Barely circulated. Brown. 10.00.

1795. Thin Planchet, "One Cent" in center of wreath. Uncirculated. Beautiful glossy light olive. A splendid cent. 35.00.

1795. Thin Planchet. "One Cent" high in wreath. Uncirculated. Light olive with traces of original red. A few letters are a little weakly struck, otherwise a splendid specimen. 20.00.

1796. Liberty Cap. Wide date. Very fine. 7.50.
1796. Fillet Head. Uncirculated. Brown. 20.00.
1796. Fillet Head. Broken die. Fine. Brown. 3.50.
1797. Uncirculated. Red. 20.00.
1797. Break in die back of head near ribbon bow. Uncirculated. Brown. 15.00.
1797. Break in die back of head near bottom of hair. Uncirculated. Brown. 15.00.
1798. Large date. Extremely fine. Brown. 5.00.
1798. Small date. Extremely fine. Light olive. 5.00.
1799. Fine for date. The date particularly fine and well struck. Desirable specimen. 35.00.

1799 over '98. Very good specimen of this variety. Light brown 20.00.

1800 over '99. Extremely fine. Hair lines scarcely touched. Good color. 5.00.
1800. Perfect date. Broken die. Extremely fine. Brown. 5.00.
1801. The curious variety with wrinkles before face. Uncirculated. Partly bright red. 20.00.
1802. Uncirculated. Beautiful light olive. 5.00.
1802. No stems to wreath. Very fine. Brown. 3.00.
1802. Curious die break under date. Uncirculated. Glossy light steel color with traces of original red. 5.00.
1802. Die broken below date. Barely touched. Handsome olive. 3.00.
1803. Large 1-100. Barest circulation. Handsome light olive. 3.00.
1803. Small 1-100. Uncirculated. Traces of brightness. 5.00.
1803. Die broken below date. But little circulated. Brown. 2.00.
1804. Broken die. Fine. 15.00.
1804. Perfect die. Fine and bold. 15.00.
1805. Uncirculated. Beautiful glossy light brown. 20.00.
1806. Barely circulated. Steel color. 25.00.
1807. Perfect date. About uncirculated. Handsome purple brown. 7.50.
1807. Perfect date. Comet variety. Very fine. Light olive. 5.00.

1807 over '06.   Fine.   Light olive.   4.00.

1808.   Scarcely circulated, but a light impression.   Light olive.   10.00.

1808.   12 star variety (so-called).   Very fine and sharp.   Brown.   5.00.

1809.   Uncirculated.   Olive.   25.00.

1810.   Perfect date.   Barely circulated.   Light olive.   7.50.

1810 over '09.   Extremely fine.   Steel color.   5.00.

1811.   Perfect date.   Quite fine.   Brown.   5.00.

1812.   Large date.   Uncirculated.   Light olive.   20.00.

1812.   Small date.   Uncirculated.   Light brown.   Very sharp.   10.00.

1813.   Uncirculated.   Brown.   7.50.

1814.   Plain 4.   Uncirculated.   Light olive.   7.50.

1814.   Cross 4.   Uncirculated.   Unusually sharp.   Handsome steel color.   7.50.

1816.   Perfect die.   Uncirculated.   Brilliant red.   3.00.

1816.   Broken die.   Uncirculated.   Brilliant red.   2.00.

1817.   Point of tiara between stars, wide date.   Uncirculated.   Bright red.   1.50.

1817.   Star near point of tiara.   Uncirculated.   Brilliant red.   2.50.

1817.   Fifteen stars.   Extremely fine.   Glossy light brown.   3.00.

1818.   Uncirculated.   Brilliant red.   .50.

1819.   Small date.   Uncirculated.   Brilliant red.   Very sharp semi-proof impression.   3.00.

1819 over '18.   Uncirculated.   Partly bright.   A few stars weak, and spot of discoloration on reverse.   1.00.

1820.   Perfect date.   2 with large curl.   Uncirculated.   Brilliant red.   3.00.

1820.   Uncirculated.   Brilliant red.   1.00.

1820 over '19.   Uncirculated.   Beautiful light olive with traces of original red.   6.00.

1821.   Not much circulated.   Glossy steel color.   7.50.

1822.   Uncirculated or barely touched.   Glossy light olive.   7.50.

1823 over '22.   Fine.   Glossy brown.   3.00.

1824.   Uncirculated.   Red and iridescent.   Handsome specimen.   25.00.

1825.   Sharp, perfect, beautiful impression.   Uncirculated.   Handsome even reddish olive.   20.00.

1826.   Uncirculated.   *Brilliant red.*   15.00.

1827. *Brilliant red proof.* 25.00.
1828. Large date. Barely circulated. Very light olive. 7.50.
1828. Small date Fine. Light brown. 3.00.
1829. *Proof impression.* Light olive with traces of red. 15.00.
1830. Small date. Sharp impression, sharp milling. Barely circulated. Beautiful purple color. 5.00.
1830. Large date. Barely circulated. Orange color. 5.00.
1831. Large letters in legend. Uncirculated. Brilliant red. 10.00.
1831. Small letters in legend. *Brilliant red proof.* 20.00.
1832. Uncirculated. Reddish olive. 10.00.
1833. Date near milling. Uncirculated. Brilliant red. 10.00.
1833. Date near head. Uncirculated. Beautiful purple brown. A gem. 5.00.
1834. Small date. Uncirculated. Handsome light olive. 5.00.
1835. Barely circulated. Handsome light olive. 5.00.
1835. Large date. Fine. Steel color. 2.00.
1836. Perfect die. Uncirculated. Light olive. 5.00.
1836. Die broken to left. Uncirculated. Glossy reddish brown. 5.00.
1836. Die broken to right. Uncirculated. Brown. 5.00.
1837. Beaded hair-string. Small letters on reverse. Proof. 12.50.
1837. Plain hair-string. Uncirculated. Brilliant red. 3.00.
1838. *Brilliant proof.* 12.50.
1838. Uncirculated. Brilliant red. 3.00.
1839. Head of 1838. Barely circulated. Greenish-olive. 3.00.
1839. Booby Head. Uncirculated. Glossy light olive. 5.00.
1839. Silly Head. Fine. Purple-brown. 1.50.
1839. Head of 1840. Extremely fine. Light brown with traces of red. 3.00.
1839 over '36. Very good. Better than usually found. 4.00.
1840. Large date. Uncirculated. Almost a brilliant proof. Glossy olive. 5.00.
1840. Small date. *Brilliant proof.* 12.50.
1840. Small date. Barest touch of circulation. Glossy light brown. 3.00.
1840. Small date. Doubly cut date. Barely circulated. Glossy light brown. 3.00.
1841. *Brilliant proof.* 20.00.
1842. Large date. Uncirculated. Light olive. 2.00.
1842. Small date. *Brilliant proof.* 25.00.
1842. Small date. Extremely fine. Light brown. 2.00.
1843. Obverse and reverse of 1842. *Brilliant proof.* 20.00.
1843. Obverse and reverse of 1842. Uncirculated. Brilliant red. 10.00.
1843. Obverse and reverse of 1844. Uncirculated. Glossy chocolate color. Almost proof surface. 7.50.
1844. *Brilliant proof.* 20.00.
1844. Uncirculated. Beautiful glossy olive brown. 3.00.

1845. Uncirculated. Purple red. 2.00.
1846. Dutch 6. Uncirculated. Brilliant red. 3.00.
1847. Uncirculated. Brilliant red. 3.00.
1848. *Brilliant proof.* 20.00.
1848. Uncirculated. Brilliant red. 3.00.
1849. *Brilliant proof.* 15.00.
1849. Uncirculated. Brilliant red. 2.00.
1850. *Brilliant proof.* 12.50.
1850. Uncirculated. Brilliant red. Beautiful specimen. Semi-proof. 1.50.
1851. Uncirculated. Brilliant red. Beautiful clean specimen. 1.00.
1852. Uncirculated. Brilliant red. Beautiful clean sharp specimen, with some proof surface. 1.50.
1853. Uncirculated. Brilliant red. Clean specimen. .75.
1854. Uncirculated. Brilliant red. Clean specimen. 1.00.
1855. Slanting 5's. *Brilliant proof.* 7.50.
1855. Straight 5's. Uncirculated. Brilliant red. Nice specimen. .75.
1856. Slanting 5. Uncirculated. Brilliant red. Nice specimen. .75.
1856. Straight 5. Uncirculated. Brilliant red. .75.
1857. Small date. *Brilliant proof.* Sharp and perfect. 7.50.
1857. Small date. Uncirculated. Brilliant red. 1.50.
1857. Large date. Uncirculated. Brilliant red. 2.00.

United States Half Cents.

1793. Uncirculated. Glossy brown. 15.00.
1794. Date close to bust. Uncirculated. Glossy steel color. 10.00.
1794. Date distant from bust. Uncirculated. Glossy light olive. 15.00.
1795. Lettered edge. About uncirculated. Light olive. 12.50.
1795. Lettered edge. Comma between 1 and 7 of date. Very fine. Glossy light brown. 5.00.
1795. Thin planchet. Uncirculated. Handsome surface. 15.00.
1797. Date close to head. About uncirculated. 6.00.
1797. Date distant from head. Fine. Brown. Broad milling. 3.00.
1797. *Lettered edge.* Very good. Rare variety. 7.50.
1800. Extra fine. Light color. 1.50.
1802. Fine. Rare in this condition. 5.00.
1804. Plain 4. Uncirculated. Handsome light olive. 1.50.

1805. No stems to wreath. Barely circulated. Light olive. 2.00.
1806. Large date. Uncirculated. Brilliant red. 1.50.
1806. Small date. No stems to wreath. Extremely fine. **Light**
olive. 1.00.
1809. Uncirculated. Handsome color. 2.50.
1810. Uncirculated. Brown. 5.00.
1811. Fine and bold. 3.00.
1825. Uncirculated. Reddish-purple. 1.50.
1826. Uncirculated. Beautiful light olive. 1.50.
1828. 12 stars. Uncirculated. Glossy light olive. 1.50.
1828. 13 stars. Uncirculated. Brilliant red. .75.
1831. With reverse similar to the 40's. Brilliant proof. 12.50.
1832. Uncirculated. Glossy light olive. 1.00.
1833. *Brilliant proof.* 5.00.
1834. *Proof.* 3.50.
1834. Uncirculated. Brilliant red. 2.00.
1835. Semi-proof. Brilliant red. 2.50.
1840. Large berries on reverse. *Brilliant proof.* 17.50.
1841. Large berries on reverse. *Brilliant proof.* 17.50.
1841. Small berries on reverse. *Brilliant proof.* 12.50.
1843. Small berries on reverse. *Brilliant proof.* 12.50.
1844. Small berries on reverse. *Brilliant proof.* 12.50.
1847. Small berries on reverse. *Brilliant proof.* 15.00.
1849. *Small date. Brilliant proof.* 15.00.
1849. Uncirculated. Mint lustre. 1.50.
1850. *Brilliant proof.* 5.00.
1851. Uncirculated. Mint lustre. .75.
1852. *Brilliant proof.* 12.50.
1853. Uncirculated. Mint lustre. .75.
1854. Uncirculated. Mint lustre. .75.
1855. *Brilliant proof.* 3.50.
1855. Uncirculated. Mint lustre. .50.
1856. *Brilliant proof.* 3.50.
1857. *Brilliant proof.* 3.50.
1857. Uncirculated. Mint lustre. .50.

Washington Coins.

1783. " Unity States" Cent. Very fine. Light olive. .75.

1783. Small head. "United States" Cent. Very fine. Brown. 1.00.

1783. Small head. "United States" Cent. *Engrilled edge.* Very rare variety. Very fine. 2.50.

Double-head Cent. Uncirculated. Glossy light brown. 2.50.

1789. Cent. Obv., head of Washington. "Geo. Washington born Virginia, Feb. 11, 1732." Rev., "Gen. of the American Armies, 1775 : Resigned 1783 : President of the United States, 1789." Very fine. Brown. Rare thus. 7.50.

1791. Cent. Large eagle. *Brilliant proof.* 6.00.

1791. Cent. Small eagle. Very fine. 5.00.

1792. Silver Half Dollar. "G. Washington President I. 1792." Very good specimen of this rare coin, but a small hole above head has been skillfully plugged. 50.00.

1792. Cent. Very good. Brown. 12.50.

1792. Cent. "Washington President 1792." The rare variety with one star above eagle's head. Extra fine, light brown color. Marred a little by several nicks on obverse. 40.00.

1793. Half-penny, rev., ship. Extra fine. Olive brown. 3.00.

Liberty and Security. Large size. Edge lettered : " An asylum for the oppress'd of all nations." Uncirculated. Bright. 3.50.

Liberty and Security. Small size. About uncirculated. Glossy brown. 2.50.

North Wales Token. Fine for piece. 1.50.

Success to U. S. Large and small sizes. Barely circulated. Nice pair. 2.50.

Funeral Medal. Reverse, skull and cross-bones. Pierced at top as usual. Silver. Good. Size 18. Rare. 5.00.

American Colonials.

SILVER.

New England Shilling. N. E.—XII. Very good. 50.00.

Maryland. Lord Baltimore Shilling, Sixpence and Fourpence. The Shilling is fine and bold, the Sixpence very good and the Fourpence fine but a little weak at right of obverse and corresponding reverse. The set is very desirable. Set for 75.00.

1783. Chalmers Annapolis Shilling. Extremely fine. 12.50.

1783. Chalmers Annapolis Sixpence. Fine. 15.00.

1783. Chalmers Annapolis Threepence. Extremely fine. A little beauty. 17.50.

1652. Massachusetts Pine Tree Shilling. Very broad planchet. Extremely fine. 15.00.

1652. Massachusetts Pine Tree Sixpence. Very fine. 10.00.

1652. Massachusetts Pine Tree Shilling. Small planchet. Very fine. 8.00.

COPPER.

1722. Rosa Americana Twopence. Good. 2.00.

1722. Rosa Americana Penny. Plain rose. Uncirculated. 5.00.

1722. Rosa Americana Penny. Vtile Dulci. Fine. 5.00.

1722. Rosa Americana Half-penny. Fine. 2.00.

1723. Rosa Americana Penny. Crowned rose. Uncirculated. 5.00.

1766. Pitt Token. "No stamps." About uncirculated. Glossy light olive. A beauty. 5.00.

1766. Pitt Token. Same as last, but appears to have been struck in pewter or a composition containing a considerable portion of that metal. About uncirculated. 5.00.

1776. Continental Currency. Tin Dollar. 2 R's in " Currency." Very fine 10.00.

1776. Continental Currency. Tin Dollar. The rare variety with only one R in " Currency." Extremely fine. 12.50.

1785. Vermonts Res Publica. Unusually good and bold. 5.00.

1786.   Vermontensium. Very fine. Light brown. 3.00.
1786.   Auctori Vermon. Baby head. Fine for piece. 3.00.
1785.   Vermon Auctori. Rev., "Immune Columbia." Always poor—this about as usually found. 5.00.
1787.   Massachusetts Cent. Horned eagle. Extremely fine. Olive color. 2.50.
1788.   Massachusetts Cent. Extremely fine. Brown. 3.00.
1787.   Massachusetts Half Cent. Uncirculated. Light olive. 3.50.
1788.   Massachusetts Half Cent. Uncirculated. Partly bright. 3.50.
1787.   Connecticut Cent. Horned Bust. Very fine. 1.00.
1787.   Connecticut Cent. "Auctori *Connect.*" Last part of "Auctori" and corresponding reverse weak, otherwise uncirculated. Light brown. 1.00.
1786.   Auctori Plebis. Plain bust. I. C. under head. Rev., "Hispanola." Large legends. Very good. Rare. 1.50.
1786.   Auctori Plebis. Draped bust. Rev., "Hispanola." Small legends. Fine. Light color. 2.00.
1786.   Auctori Plebis. Draped bust. Larger legend. Reverse seems to be plain or extremely weakly struck. Fine. 1.50.
1787.   New York Cent. "Liber Natus Libertatem Defendo." Indian with tomahawk and bow. Rev., Arms of New York, "Excelsior" below. Very good or fine excepting that a small hole at Indian's feet has been plugged. Extremely rare. 25.00.
1787.   New York Cent. Arms of New York, "Excelsior" below; rev., eagle. Very good. 20.00.
1787.   Nova Eborac. Seated figure to right. Very fine. Light brown. 4.00.
1787.   Nova Eborac. Seated figure to left. Fine. 3.00.
1787.   Nova Eborac. The extremely rare variety with two quatrefoils before "Nova." Nearly fine. Light brown. 10.00.
1794.   Talbot, Allum & Lee. John Howard reverse. Very fine. Brown. 1.50.
1795.   Talbot, Allum & Lee. Uncirculated. Light olive. 2.00.
Kentucky Cent. Thin planchet. Uncirculated. 2.00.
Kentucky Cent. Lettered edge. Uncirculated. Glossy olive. Semi-proof surface. 3.00.
1787.   Immunis Columbia. Liberty seated on globe. Fine. Light color. 6.00.
1787.   Franklin Cent. "Mind your business." Rev., "States United." Uncirculated. Bright red. .75.
1787.   Franklin Cent. Same, but reverse, "United States." Uncirculated. Bright red. Planchet a little defective. Rare. 1.25.
New Jersey. St. Patrick Halfpence ("Mark Newby"). St. Patrick showing shamrock to people. Large and small letters in legend. Fine pair. Brown color. Pair for 8.00.

New Jersey. St. Patrick Farthings. St. Patrick banishing the snakes from Ireland. Fine specimens from 7 different dies. Set of 7 pieces for 10.00.

1786. New Jersey. 12–G. *No coulter*. A light impression, but really uncirculated. Light olive with traces of red. 5.00.

1786. New Jersey. 12–I. *No coulter*. Good. Rare. 3.00.

1788. New Jersey. 50–f. Horse head to left. Very fine. 5.00.

1773. Virginia Half Cent. Uncirculated. Brilliant red. .75.

North Carolina Token (so-called). Ship; rev., shield, 13 stars. Brass. Uncirculated. 1.25.

1783. Nova Constellatio. Almost uncirculated. 1.00.

1783. Nova Constellatio (sic). Club rays. Extremely fine. Brown. 1.00.

1785. Nova Constellatio. Very fine. Olive color. 1.00.

James II. Tin Plantation Piece. Pewter. Barely circulated. 2.50.

United States Patterns.

1792. Disme. Silver. Fine. Only one other known in silver, and the date is rubbed off of that piece. 125.00.

1792. Martha Washington Half Disme. Very fine. 15.00.

1792. Silver-Centre Cent. Head of Liberty facing to right. LIBERTY PARENT OF SCIENCE & INDUSTRY. Rev., ONE CENT in wreath, $\frac{1}{100}$ below. UNITED STATES OF AMERICA. This specimen is struck on a full copper planchet—no hole for silver centre—and is rarer than the silver centre specimens. I know of no duplicate. Barely circulated. Dark olive. 100.00.

1838. Half Dollar. Liberty seated. Rev., flying eagle. Silver proof. 25.00.

1838. Half Dollar. Liberty seated. Rev., standing eagle. Silver proof. 25.00.

1838. Half Dollar. Head of Liberty. Rev., flying eagle. Silver, nearly proof. 4.00.

1838. Half Dollar. Head of Liberty. Rev., standing eagle. Silver proof. 7.50.

1839. Half Dollar. Nude bust of Liberty facing to *right*. Reverse same as regular issue of 1839–1841. Silver proof. 35.00.

1839. Half Dollar. Same as last, but with reverse of 1842–1865. Silver proof. 35.00.

1839. Half Dollar. Same as last. Copper proof. 5.00.

1849. Three Cents. Obv., same as ½ Dime. Silver proof. 5.00.

1850. Three Cents. Liberty cap in rays. Brilliant proof. 3.50.

1850. Ring Cent. No hole; rev., blank. Silver alloy. .75.

1853. Cent. Liberty head. Nickel. Dull proof. 1.00.

———. Blank obverse. Reverse same as last. Nickel proof. .50.

1854. Cent. Head of Liberty without stars. Bronze proof. 1.00.

1855. Cent. Flying eagle. Bronze proof. 1.00.

(1856). Flying eagle. No date or legend. Copper proof. 2.00.

1857. Cent. Head of Liberty; rev., "One Cent" in wreath. Nickel proof. 3.00.

1858. Half Dollar. Obverse of regular issue. Reverse, Paquette's design with motto-ribbon in eagle's beak. Silver. Dull proof. 20.00.

1858. Quarter Dollar. Obverse of regular issue. Reverse, Paquette's design—no ribbon. Silver proof. 15.00.

1858. Cents. Set of twelve patterns. Indian head, large and small eagles, each with four reverses. 10.00.

1858. Cent. Indian head. Nickel proof. 1.00.

1859. Liberty Head. Reverses, "½ dollar," "Half dollar," "50 cents"—also, Liberty seated. Silver proofs. Set of 4 pieces for 6.00.

1859. Quarter Dollar. Obverse of regular issue. Reverse, Paquette's design—no motto-ribbon. Silver proof. 7.50.

1859. Cent. Regular issue; rev., oak wreath and shield. Uncirculated. 1.00.

1861. Half Dollar. Rev's., "God our Trust" in field above eagle on reverse, and "God our Trust" on label. Brilliant proofs. Pair for 7.50.

1862. Half Dollar. Rev.'s., "God our Trust" in field above eagle on reverse, and "God our Trust" on label. Brilliant proofs. Pair for 5.00.

1863. Half Dollar. Rev's., "God our Trust" in field above eagle on reverse, and "God our Trust" on label. Brilliant proofs. Pair for 7.50.

1863. Pattern Three Cents. Obverse same as old copper cent; rev., 3 cents in wreath. Copper proof. 2.50.

1863. Pattern Three Cents. Same as last. Aluminum proof. 5.00.

1863. Pattern Two Cents. Head of Washington. Rev., similar to regular issue, but "Cents" more curved. Aluminum proof. 3.00.

1863.   Pattern Two Cents.   Same as last, but thinner planchet. Aluminum proof.   3.00.

1863.   Pattern Two Cents.   Same as last.   Nickel proof.   3.00.

1863.   Pattern Two Cents.   Same as last.   Copper proof.   1.50.

1863.   Pattern Two Cents.   Similar to issue of 1864, but with reverse like last, "Cents" curved.   Copper proof.   1.50.

1863.   Pattern Two Cents.   Same as last, but thin planchet.   Copper proof.   1.50.

1863.   Pattern Two Cents.   Same as last.   Nickel proof.   3.00.

1863.   Cent.   Thin planchet.   Copper proof.   1.00.

1864.   Quarter Dollar.   Obverse of regular issue.   Rev., smaller eagle with long arrows.   Silver proof.   7.50.

1864.   Cent.   Obverse of regular type; reverse is obverse of 1858 eagle cent, small legend.   Nickel proof.   5.00.

1865.   Quarter Dollar.   Obverse of regular issue.   Rev., smaller eagle with long arrows.   Silver proof.   7.50.

1865.   Five Cents.   Type adopted in 1867—no bars.   Nickel proof. Extremely rare.   15.00.

1865.   Two Cents.   Regular issue, but in an alloy containing a large proportion of nickel.   Proof.   1.50.

1866.   Five Cents.   Head of Lincoln.   Rev., Value in wreath. Nickel proof.   20.00.

1866.   Five Cents.   Head of Lincoln.   Copper proof.   10.00.

1866.   Five Cents.   Head of Washington, "In God we Trust." Rev., 5 in wreath.   Nickel proof.   1.50.

1866.   Five Cents.   Obv., same as last; rev., same as regular issue. Nickel proof.   1.50.

1866.   Five Cents.   Obverse same as regular issue.   Reverse, large 5 in wreath.   Nickel proof.   1.50.

1866.   Five Cents.   Same as last, but small 5 in wreath.   Nickel proof.   1.50.

1866.   Five Cents.   Obverse same as regular issue except that the date is separated by a ball; reverse, 5 in wreath. Nickel proof.   1.50.

1867.   Five Cents.   Head of Liberty.   Rev., "5 cents" in wreath, "Cents" straight.   Nickel proof.   .75.

1867.   Five Cents.   Same as last, but "Cents" curved.   Nickel proof.   .75.

1867.   Five Cents.   Same as last, but the reverse is the regular issue without bars.   Nickel proof.   10.00.

1867.   Cent.   Pure nickel.   Uncirculated.   1.50.

1867.   Five Cents.   Longacre's design.   Profile to left with long plumes.   Rev., V. on shield.   Aluminum proof.   Rare.   1.50.

1868.   Ten Cents.   Obverse same as old copper cent.   Nickel proof.   5.00.

1868.   Ten Cents.   Same as last.   Copper proof.   2.50.

1868.   Dime.   Large star above and date below "One Dime" on reverse.   Silver proof.   2.50.

1868. One, Three, Five Cents. Liberty head. Nickel proofs. 2.00.

1869. 50, 25, and 10 Cents. Draped head of Liberty, with Phrygian cap; another bust with plain diadem; another with star on forehead. Three of each value. Reeded edges. Silver proofs. Set of 9 pieces. 7.50.

1869. Similar set. Aluminum proofs. 5.00.

1869. Dimes. "Sil. 6, Nic. 1," and "Sil., Nic., Cop." Proofs. Pair 2.00.

1869. Five Cents. Large V on shield. Nickel proof. 1.50.

1869. Three Cents. Nickel. Dull proof. .50.

1870. 50, 25, and 10 Cents. Draped head of Liberty, with Phrygian cap; another bust with plain diadem; another with star on forehead. Three of each value. "Standard" in small letters on reverse. Reeded edges. Silver proofs. Set of 9 pieces. 7.50.

1870. Similar set. Aluminum proofs. 5.00.

1870. Similar set but "Standard Silver" in large letters. Silver proofs. 10.00.

1870. Similar to last. Aluminum proofs. 7.50.

1870. Longacre's Dollar. Indian queen. Silver proof. 20.00.

1870. Barber's beautiful patterns. Liberty seated with shield, and pole with cap. Values on reverse in figures within a wreath of cotton, corn and sugar. "Standard" above. Plain edges. $1, 50c., 25c., 10c., 5c. Silver proofs. Set for 40.00.

1870. Same. Reeded edge except the 5 and 10 cents. Copper proofs. 7.50.

1870. Same. Plain edges. Copper proofs. 7.50.

1870. Same, including a 3 cent piece. Reverse same as the regular issue. Reeded edges. Copper proofs. 7.50.

1870. Same as last. Dollar, half, quarter, dime and half-dime. Plain edges. Silver proofs. Set for 30.00.

1870. Same as last. Dollar, half, quarter and dime. All plain edges. Copper proofs. 5.00.

1871. Longacre's dollar, half, quarter, dime and half dime. Indian queen. Rev., 1 Dollar, etc., "Standard" above. Silver proofs. The dollar excessively rare. Set 50.00.

1871. Longacre's Indian Queen Dollar. Rev., same as regular issue. Silver proof. 25.00.

1871. Five Cents. Head of Liberty. Rev., "5 Cents" in wreath. Nickel proof. 2.00.

1871. Five Cents. Head of Liberty. Rev., "V Cents" in wreath. Nickel proof. 2.00.

1872. Barber's $1, 50 cts., 25 cts. Amazonian figure of Liberty seated caressing an eagle. Silver proofs. Set 50.00.

1873. Set of the six rare pattern Trade Dollars. Splendid proofs. 30.00.

1873. Trade Dollar. The rare pattern with long plow handles. Silver proof. 25.00.

1874. International Coinage. Head of Liberty, " United States of America " above. Rev., 16.72 Grams. 900 Fine. Ubique," surrounded by labels " 10 Dollars," " Sterling £2. 1. 1.," etc. Copper proof. Rare. 5.00.

1874. Twenty Cents. Female seated on globe. Silver proof. 20.00.

1874. Twenty Cents. Female seated on globe. Copper proof. 5.00.

1875. Twenty Cents. Female seated on globe, holds olive branch, steamship at sea. Silver proof. 12.50.

1875. Twenty Cents. Head of Liberty ; reverse, " 20" on shield. Silver proof. 12.50.

1875. Twenty Cents. Same as regular issue, but with reverse " ½ of a dollar." Silver proof. 12.50.

1877. Half Dollars. Head of Liberty in circle of pellets, " E Plurius Unum" above, date below, 7 stars to right, 6 to left. Reverses of Maris sale, Nos. 198, 199, 200. Copper proofs. 3 pcs. 7.50.

1877. Half Dollar. Head of Liberty with broad band inscribed " Liberty." 13 stars. Rev., Maris sale No. 204. Small eagle on large shield. Copper proof. 2.50.

1878. Goloid Metric Dollar. Brilliant proof. 10.00.

1878. Barber's beautiful pattern for the Standard Dollar. The rejected design, which was handsomer than the one by Morgan accepted. Also, the original Morgan design with only 3 leaves to branch under eagle's feet. Brilliant proofs. Pair for 15.00.

1879. Double Eagle. Has " 30 G. 1.5 S. 3.5 C. 35 grams 1879," separated by stars on obverse around Liberty head ; rev., same as regular issue. Gold proof. Only 3 struck. 100.00.

1879. Silver metric and goloid dollars. Brilliant proofs. Pair for 4.00.

1881. One, Three. Five Cents. Obverse similar to adopted designs ; rev., value in Roman numerals in corn and oak wreath. Nickel proofs. 3.50.

1882. Five Cents. Obverse and reverse same as regular issue without " Cents," excepting in date. Nickel proof. 3.50.

1882. Five Cents. " United States of America" around head. Reverse, V in corn and oak wreath, " E Pluribus Unum" above. Nickel proof. 3.50.

1882. Same as the regular issue of this year (old design), except that the shield on reverse is large and has no boll at bottom. Extremely rare. Nickel proof. 5.00.

1883. Five Cents. Same as the regular issue, excepting a band inscribed " Cents" on reverse over V. Nickel proof. 3.5.0

1883. Five Cents. Same as regular issue without " Cents," but has word " Liberty" above head on obverse. Nickel proof. 3.50.

1883.   Five Cents. Obverse, Liberty head surrounded by "United States of America." Reverses have a wreath of corn, cotton and sugar surrounded by 13 stars, 6 to right, 7 to left, "Five" above, "Cents" below. In the center is the percentage of metal: "50 N. 50 C.," "33 N. 67 C.," and "Pure Nickel." Nickel proofs. Set of 3 pieces. 25.00.

Confederate Notes.

$100.   1861. Montgomery. Train of cars to right. Fine. 10.00.
$100.   1861. Richmond. Train of cars to left. Uncirculated. 15.00.
$50.   1861. Montgomery. Negroes hoeing cotton. Uncirculated. 7.50.
1864.   Set from 50 cts. to $500. 1.25.

Foreign Crowns and Multiples of Crowns.

(All of crown size unless otherwise stated.)

Austria.   1549.   Ferdinand I. Fine. 3.50.
1558.   Ferdinand I. With title as Duke of Burgundy. Fine. 3.50.
1592.   Rudolph II. Extremely fine. 3.00.
1603.   Maximilian. As Grand Master of Teutonic Knights. Uncirculated. 3.50.
1610.   Rudolph II. Very fine. 3.00.
1612.   Mathias II. Uncirculated. 3.50.
1617.   Ferdinand II. Very fine. 2.50.
1621.   Leopold. Uncirculated. Brilliant mint lustre. 3.50.
1631.   Ferdinand II. Broad Crown. Fine. 2.50.
——.   Archduke Ferdinand Charles. *Double Crown.* Extremely fine. 6.50.
1638.   Ferdinand III. Extremely fine. 2.50.
1640.   Ferdinand III. *Double Crown.* Uncirculated. 7.50.
1656.   Ferdinand III. Fine. 2.50.
1660.   Leopold. Very fine. 2.50.
——.   Leopold and Claudia de Medici. *Double Crown.* Uncirculated. Brilliant mint lustre. 7.50.
1683.   Broad Sede-Vacante Crown. Double-headed eagle on world, crescent in clouds. Barely circulated. 3.00.
1690.   Leopold the Hogmouth. Broad Crown. Extremely fine. 2.50.
1701.   Leopold the Hogmouth. Uncirculated. 3.00.
Augsburg.   1625.   Ferdinand II. Saint above pine cone. Uncirculated. Brilliant mint lustre. 3.50.
1643.   Ferdinand III. View of city and pine cone on reverse. Uncirculated. Brilliant mint lustre. 3.50.
Brandenburg.   1549.   Albert. Fine. 3.50.
Brunswick.   1562.   Henry. Rev., arms supported by a wild man. Fine. Rare. 5.00.
15)78.   Eric. Shield before wild man is surrounded by the order of the Golden Fleece. Fine. Very rare. 5.00.

1595. Henry Julius. Rebel Dollar. Wild man with torch and spear, dog behind. The reverse represents the swallowing up of Korah, Dathan and Abiram and biblical reference below : NUME XVI. For description of this interesting and rare piece, see American Joúrnal of Numismatics, Vol. IV., page 74. Fine. 5.00.

1597 Henry Julius. "Truth" Crown. Scene of crucifixion. "Veritas" above. Fine. 3.00.

1599. Henry Julius. "Wasp" Crown. Lion and wasps. Very fine. 5.00.

——. Augustus. "Ship" Crown. Uncirculated. 5.00.

1624. Christian. Uncirculated. 3.50.

1643. Augustus. " Bell " Crown. Three hands pulling bell. "*Ano.* 1643." Very fine. 3.50.

1643. Augustus. " Bell " Crown. "*Ao.* 1643." Fine. 3.00.

1662. Christian. "Horse" Crown. Fine. 3.50.

1685. Rudolph Augustus. *Broad Triple Crown.* Female playing the lute, standing on a snail, mining scene and landscape in distance. Uncirculated. 30.00.

1687 Ernest Augustus. $\frac{2}{3}$ Crown. Wild man. Uncirculated. Rare. 3.50.

1688. Rudolph Augustus and Anton Ulrich. Busts jugata. *Broad Crown.* About uncirculated. 4.00.

1716. Augustus William. Wild man holding pine tree. Fine. 3.00.

Basle. *Broad Double Crown.* View of the city. Extremely fine. 6.50.

Brabant. 1567. Extremely fine. 3.50.

1622. Philip IV. Fine. 2.50.

1658. Philip IV. Very fine. 2.50.

Bavaria. 1625. Maximilian. Virgin and Child. Rev., Arms of the Palatinate. Extremely fine. 2.50.

Campen. 1597. Date between turrets of castle. Very good. 2.50.

Denmark. 1659. Frederick III. Sword dividing hand, date Feb. 2nd. Extremely fine. Very rare. 3.50.

Genoa. 1631. Conrad II. (King of the Romans). Broad $1\frac{1}{2}$ Crown. Very fine. Rare. 5.00.

1665. Thick Double Crown. Fine. 4.00.

1687. Virgin and Child. Broad Double Crown. Small hole at top. Very fine. 3.50.

Hamburg. 1600–1700. Marriage Triple Crown. Man and woman, hands joined. Extremely fine. 10.00.

1600–1700. Broad Baptismal Double Crown. Scene of Baptism in Jordan. Extremely fine. 5.00.

Hungary. 1556. Ferd. I. Very fine. 3.50.

Holland. 1682. *Triple Crown.* Knight on horseback. Uncirculated. Brilliant mint lustre. 10.00.

Hesse. 1631. "Whirlwind" Crown. Fine. 3.50.

Luneberg. 1548. Profile in Crescent. Fine. Very rare. 5.00.

Mantua. Charles I. Rev., Sun progressing through signs of Zodiac, stars in field, world below. Extremely fine. Rare. 5.00.

Mansfield. 1624. Wolfgang John George. Very good. 2.00.

Netherlands. 1790. Insurrection Crown. Lion with sword and shield. Proof. 4.00.

Poland. 1727. Frederick Augustus. Mortuary $\frac{2}{3}$ Crown. In honor of Christina, Queen of Poland. Cypress between pyramid of hearts. Fine. 2.00.

Parma. 1627. Odoardo Farnese. Rev., bust of St. Antonius as a Roman soldier. Extremely fine. 3.00.

1631. Odoardo Farnese. Rev., St. Antonius carrying standard. Uncirculated. 3.50.

Presburg. 1716. Wolfgang. Uncirculated. 2.50.

Russia. 1762. Peter III. Only reigned 6 months. Very good. 3.00.

Salzburg. 1552. Michael. Very fine. 3.50.

1593. *Square Double Crown.* Four heads blowing wind against a tower. Fine. 7.50.

1621. St. Rupert seated. Uncirculated. Mint lustre. 3.00.

1628. Two bishops holding up cathedral; rev., procession of priests carrying religious emblems. Very fine. 3.00.

1630. Uncirculated. Brilliant mint lustre. 3.00.

1708. John Ernest. Uncirculated. Brilliant mint lustre. 2.50.

St. Gall. 1624. " Bear Crown." Fine. 3.00.

Schaffhausen. 1621. Ram springing from temple door. Very good. 2.50.

Schwarzenberg 1696. Ferdinand and Maria Anna. Busts jugate. Very fine. 2.50.

Spain. 1558. Philip of Spain, with title as King of Spain and England. Fine. 3.50.

Saxony. 1537. John Fred. and George. Very fine. 3.50.

1540. John Fred.; rev., bust of Henry. Nearly uncirculated. 4.00.

1583. John and Fred. Wm. Bust on each side. Good. 2.50.

1593. " Three Dukes." Quarter Crown. Fine. 1.00.

1598. " Three Dukes " Crown. Very fine. 3.00.

1602. John Casimer and John Ernest. Busts facing. Barely circulated. 3.00.

1606. Christian II. with drawn sword; rev., busts of John George and Augustus facing. Very fine. 2.50.

1615. John George. Square Double Crown. Fine. 6.00.

1620. " Four Dukes " Crown. Three busts in procession; rev., bust. Uncirculated. 3.50.

1624. Busts of Wm., Fred. and Fred. Ernest. Barely circulated. 3.50.

1625 John George. Bust with drawn sword. Barely circulated. 3.50.

1630. John George. Half crown, Crown and Double Crown. Centennial of Augsburg Confession. An almost uncirculated set. 12.50.

1635. John George. Fine. 2.50

1652. John George. Uncirculated. Mint lustre. 3.50.

1661. John George II. Broad Double Crown (over 2½ in. in diameter). Monument. To left; open book, crowned, with snake on cross and Christ on cross—to right; crossed swords and cap. Uncirculated. A beauty. 15.00.

Sicily. 1732. Charles III. *Triple Crown.* Bust with curls to right. Rev., Phoenix. Uncirculated. Brilliant mint lustre. 15.00.

Transylvania. 1591. Three boar tusks on reverse. Uncirculated. 3.50.

Tuscany. 1665. Ferdinand II. Rev., rose bush. Fine. Rare. 3.00.

1671. Max. Henry. Nearly uncirculated. Mint lustre. 3.00.

1676. Cosmos III. Rev., Baptism in Jordan. Fine. 2.50.

Venice. John Cornaro I. (1625–1630.) Lion of St. Mark on shield. Very good. 2.50.

1683. Aloysius Contarino, Doge. St. Martin and the beggar. Exceedingly fine. Size 23. 3.00.

Paolo Reneir. (1779–1789). Dollar. Doge with standard kneeling before St. Mark. Rev., Lion before castle. Uncirculated. 3.50.

Wittenberg. 1661. Reformation Crown. Bust of Luther; rev., view of the city. Nearly uncirculated. Rare. 4.00.

West Frisia. 1596. *Double Crown.* Neptune on sea monster. Very good. 6.00.

1601. Lions. *Double Crown.* Uncirculated. 10.00.

Zug. 1621. Extremely fine. 3.50.

Zealand. 1642. Very good. 2.50.

1664. 2⅓ Crown. Crowned eagle with bunch of arrows; rev., sun (IHS in centre) and crescent. Extremely fine. Rare. 3.00.

Silver Siege and Necessity Coins.

Breda. 1625. Diamond shape. Size 14. Very fine. 2.50.

Carthagena. 1873. 2 and 5 Pesetas. Struck while the Centralists besieged the city. Uncirculated. Very rare. Pair for 6.00.

Campen. 1578. Siege Crown of 42 Stubers. Arms of the city, CAMPEN, 42 ST., 1578. Diamond shape. Fine and rare. 7.50.

Gotha. 1567. Siege crown. Very fine. 3.50.

Haarlem. 1572. Oblong. Size 16x20. Fine. Very rare. 4.00.

Leyden. 1574. Siege Crown. Lion grasping staff with liberty cap; rev., arms of the city, N. O. V. L. S. G. I. P. A. C., or "Money of the besieged city of Leyden, struck under the most illustrious governor, the Prince of Orange." Sharp, uncirculated, very rare and interesting. 7.50.

Majorca. 1821. Ferd. VII. Siege Dollar. Uncirculated. 3.00.

Middleburg. 1572. Square Siege Crown. Extremely fine. 5.00.

Munster. 1660. Square Siege Crown. Extremely fine. 5.00.

Minden. 1624. Oblong Siege Coin for 8 Groschen. Very fine. 2.00.

Nurnberg. 1650. Diamond-shaped Peace Klippe. Hand with wreath over globe. Uncirculated. Size 20. 2.50.

Saragossa. 1809. Ferd. VII. Siege Dollar. Uncirculated. 3.00.

Salzburg. 1651, 1656. Klippes (diamond shaped) for one-sixth and one-ninth Crown. Very fine. Pair, 2.50.

Jewish Coins.

Simon Maccabeus. B. C. 143. Half Shekel Cup of manna; rev., a triple lily or hyacinth. Very fine, but slight erosion on obverse. 15.00.

John Hyrancus. B. C. 136. *Widow's Mite.* Good. Very rare. 2.50.

Herod the Great. B. C. 37. *Widow's Mite.* Fair. 2.00.

Under Roman Procurator. A. D. 14. *Widow's Mite.* Date palm. Good. 2.00.

Herod Agrippa II. A. D. 37. (The Herod the King of Acts xii. 1.) *Mite.* Wheat heads and royal umbrella. Fine. 2.00.

Claudius Felix, Procurator under Nero. *Mite.* A palm branch; rev., wreath. Very good, but edge nicked. 1.50.

Vespasian. A. D. 70. Denarius. Rev., captive beside armor, " Judæa " below. Struck to commemorate the destruction of Jerusalem. The finest specimen I have seen in a long time. 6.00. Another. fine. 3.00.

Vespasian. A. D. 70. Great bronze. Rev., captive under tree, soldier watching, " Judæa Capta." Very good. 7.50.

Roman Bronze, etc.

Aes. Early type. B. C. 500. Double head of Janus; rev., prow. Weight 9 oz. Very good. 7.50.

Quadrans. Early type. Boar on each side. Fine. 2.50.

Sextans. Early type. Head of Minerva; rev., prow. Fine. 2.50.
Aes. Reduced type. Double head of Janus; rev., prow. Fine. 1.50.
Semis. Reduced type. Head of Jupiter; rev., prow. Very fine. 1.00.
Egypt. Large Bronze. Head of Jupiter; rev., eagle. Fine. Size 28. Weight 3¼ oz. 2.50.
Egypt. Similar. Size 25. Fine. Weight 1¾ oz. 1.50.
Turkuman. Youluk-Arslan. A. D. 1180. Khalefeh, squatted, holds sword up-lifted in right hand and male head in left. Fine. 1.25.
Youluk-Arslau. A. D. 1180. Bust facing in square. Fine. 1.00.
Ortokides Dynasty. Golbeddin el Ghazı. A. D. 1176. Large and small busts; rev., cuneiform characters. Fine. 1.00.
Mahmoud Benu Zengee. A. D. 1223. Head facing. Fine. 1.00.
Similar to last. Caliphs of Bagdad. Heads and squatting figures. Good to fine, one pierced. 7 pcs. 2.50.
Herculaneum. Lead coins from ruins. As usually found. 8 pcs. 2.00.
Augustus and Agrippa. Rev., crocodile chained to palm tree. COL. NEM. (Colony Nemausus). Very fine. 2.00.

Roman Silver Denarii.

Pompey the Great. Born 106 B. C. Head between lituus and vase. Very good. 3.50.
M. Junius Brutus. Head of Liberty; rev., trophy, BRUTUS IMP. Very fine. 3.00.
M. Junius Brutus. Head, "Libertas." Rev., procession of lictors, BRUTUS below. Very fine. 2.50.
Julius Cæsar. Struck about 47 B. C. Head of Ceres. "Cos Tert Dict Iter." (Consul third time; Dictator second time). Rev., pontifical implements. Extremely fine. 3.50.
Julius Cæsar. "Cæsar Dict. Perpetuo." Veiled head of Cæsar; rev., Venus Ni-cephore standing holding a victory and hasta. Very good. 2.50.
Julius Cæsar. Head of Venus to right; rev., two Gaulish captives under a trophy "Cæsar" below. Uncirculated. 3.50.
Julius Cæsar. Laureated head of Apollo; rev., prætor drawing two oxen. "IMP CÆSAR." Very fine. 3.50.
Julius Cæsar. Elephant trampling a serpent; rev., religious implements. Uncir-culated. Brilliant mint lustre. 2.50.
Mark Anthony. War galley; rev., standards, LEG V. Good. .75.
Augustus Cæsar. B. C. 31. Youthful head. "C. Cæsar III." Uncirculated 3.00.
Tiberius. A. D. 14. "Tribute penny." Very good. 2.00.
Galba. A. D. 68. Good. 1.00.
Otho. A. D. 69. Fine and rare. 3.00.
Vitellius. A. D. 69. Fine and rare. 3.00.
Vespasian. A. D. 70. Extremely fine. 1.50.
Titus. A. D. 79. Very good. Scarce. 1.50.
Domitian. A. D. 81. Fine. 1.00.
Nerva. A. D. 96. Very good. 1.00.
Trajan. A. D. 98. Extremely fine. 1.50.
Hadrian. A. D. 117. *Double Denarius.* Very good. Rare. 2.00.
Hadrian. A. D. 117. Rev., star and crescent. Very good. 1.00.
Antonius Pius. A. D. 138. Very fine. 1.00.
Septimus Severus. A. D. 193. Barely circulated. 1.00.
Geta. A. D. 211. Fine. .75.
Elagabalus. A. D. 218. About uncirculated. 1.00.
Severus Alexander. A. D. 222. Extremely fine. 1.00.
Philip the Arab. A. D. 244. Extremely fine. .75.

Ancient Greek Coins.

Tetradrachms. Athens. Archaic style. 525 B. C. Head of Athena; rev., owl. Very fine. 5.00.

Macedonia. Philip III. Type of Alexander the Great. Very good but test cut on edge. 2.00.

Alexander the Great. 336 B. C. *As it dropped from the die.* The sharpest and handsomest specimen I have seen. 15.00. Another, very good, 3.50.

Macedonia as a Roman province. 158 B. C. Shield, centre of which is bust of Artemis; rev., club in wreath. Obv., fair; rev., fine. 1.50.

Same. 89 B. C. Head of Alexander the Great with flowing hair and Ammon horn, "Macedon" below. Rev., club, money chest and chair in wreath, with name of the Roman Quaestor Aesillas. Very fine. 5.00.

Side, Pamphylia. 190 B. C. Fine helmeted head; rev., winged Nike with wreath. Very fine. 5.00.

Syracuse. 400 B. C. Head of Arethusa surrounded by dolphins. Rev., Victory in biga. Very good. 4.00.

Thrace. 146 B. C. Head of the young Dionysos; rev., Hercules with club. Very broad planchet, rude design. Very fine. 2.50.

Tyre. 126 B. C. Head of Hercules; rev., eagle. Fine. 5.00.

Egypt. One of the earlier Ptolemies. Very good. 3.50.

Ptolemy XIII. 79 B. C. Fine. 3.50.

Didrachms. Aegina. Earliest period. 700 B. C. Turtle; rev., punch marks. Fine. 5.00.

Agrigentum. 472 B. C. Sea eagle and crab. Fine. 2.00.

Boeotia. 379 B. C. Shield; rev., amphora. Very good. 2.50.

Chios. 500 B. C. Seated griffin; rev., punch marks. Fine. 4.00.

Caulonia. 480 B. C. Nude slinger and stag; rev., stag. Fine. 2.50.

Crotona. 550 B. C. Tripod, stork; rev., incused. Fine. 3.50.

Gela. 466 B. C. Man-headed bull; rev., horseman. Fine. 3.50.

Metapontum. 550 B. C. Broad Didrachm. Ear of wheat; the same incused. Fine. 5.00.

Neapolis. Venus. Rev., minotaur. Fine. 2 00.

Posidonia. Neptune; rev., bull. Very good. 1.50.

Sybaris. 550 B. C. Broad Didrachm. Bull with head turned back; rev., same incused. Fine. 7.50.

Tarentum. 360 B. C. Naked horseman; rev., Taras on dolphin. Extremely fine. 2.50.

Thasos. 465 B. C. Satyr on knee bearing a nymph in his arms; rev., punch mark. Fine. 5.00.

Thurium. Minerva; rev., bull. Very fine. 4 00.

Velia. 400 B. C. Head of Pallas; rev., lion devouring a skull. Fine. 2.50.

Egypt. Ptolemy VIII. 146 B. C. Didrachm. Head; rev., eagle. Fine. 2.00.

Drachms. Cnidus. Thick. Head of Venus in sunken square; rev., lion's head. Fine. 2.00.

Dyrrhachium. Cow suckling calf. Very fine. 2.00.

Spain. Head; rev., horseman. Very good. 1.00.

Sybaris. 530 B. C. Bull; rev., incused. Very good. 2.50.

Hemi-Drachms. Aegina. 700 B. C. Earliest period. Tortoise; rev., punch mark. Very good. 2.50.

Cherosonesus. Forepart of lion. Fine. .75.

Caria. Lion's head and star. Very fine. 1.00.

Histiaea. Bacchante head; rev., female on prow. Extremely fine. 1.00.

Macedonia. Philip II. Head; rev., horseman. Very good. 1.00.

Messana. Hare. Fine. 1.00.

Miletas. Head; rev., lion. Fine. .50.

Phocis. Bull's head. Fine. 1.25.

Rhodes. An early type. Head; rev., flower in incused square. Very good. 1.00.

Sinope. Head; rev., harpy eagle. Good. .50.

Sicyon. Lion and dove. Good. .50.

Thurium. Head; rev., bull. Very good. .75.

Persia. Darius I. 521 B. C. King as an archer. Rev., punch mark. Silver Daric. Very good. Rare. 5.00.

Sassanides. Broad Drachm. Size 21. Very fine. 1.50.

Sassanides. Small Drachm. Very fine. 1.00.

Peace Medals.

Libertas Americana. 1783. Beautiful head of Liberty with cap and pole; rev. Gallia protecting America from attacks of British lion. Size 30. Bronze proof. 3.50.

Libertas Americana. 1783. Louis XVI. on throne pointing to an American shield which a female is hanging on a pillar surmounted by a liberty cap; rev., Minerva holding shield. Tin. Very good. Size 29. Rare. 1.50.

Louis XVIII ; rev., pedestal, America and France on either side; "Gallia et America fœderata, etc." Bronze proof. Size 32. 1.50.

1781. Netherlands. Four shields linked, "Gewapende Neutraliteit;" rev., "Jehovah," etc., in ten lines. Silver. Dull proof. 2.50.

Figure of Netherlands standing ; " Netherland declares America free." Rev., a staff bearing flags of Holland and U. S., bales of goods and ship. " The Universal Wish, 1782." Silver proof. Size 22. 5.00.

Washington Medals.

Manly medal. Bust with aged features. "Geo. Washington, born Virginia Feb. 11, 1732." Rev., " General of American Armies 1775, resigned 1783, President of United States 1789." Original. Copper. Good. Size 31. 2.00.

Eccleston medal, Lancaster, 1805. Bust to right; rev., Indian with bow and arrow and " The land was ours " encircled by three lines of inscription. Bronze. Very fine, but lightly nicked. Size 48. 3.50.

Bust to left ; George Washington, by F. B. Smith & Hartmann, N. Y.; rev., tomb of Washington; above, Fame flying. Bronze proof. Rare. Size 41. 5.00.

Bust to right, Paquet; rev., cabinet of Washington medals in U. S. Mint. Bronze, proof. Size 38. 1.25.

Bust, cherry tree scene, wood, size 36. .35.

Rare silver temperance token by Bale, size 12, pierced. 1.00.

Westwood medal. Bust to right; rev., " Made commander-in-chief," etc. Bronze. Size 26. 5.00.

Head to left. George Washington. Rev., " Born Feb. 22d, 1732," etc., in 6 lines. Silver proof. Weight 2 oz. Size 29. 3.00.

Liberty crowning bust of Washington on pedestal. Rev., Benevolence helping fallen man. 1808. Washington Benevolent Society, New York. Silver. Dull proof. Size 27. 2.00.

Washington. Rev., sword and fasces on altar. The Halliday medal. Very fine. Size 34. 2.50.

Bust ; reverses, the different battles of 1776. Set of 8 pieces. Copper proofs. Size 22. 3.00.

Presidential Medals.

James Madison. Original *silver* peace medal. Bust to left ; rev., clasped hands, pipe above. Pierced at top for suspension and has evidently been worn by the Indian who received it. Very fine and rare. Size 48. Weighs 5¾ oz. Av. 15.00.

Same. Bronze proof. Size 48. 1.50.

Same. Bust to right ; rev., eagle, scroll, etc., w. m. proof. Size 40. 1.00.

James Monroe. Peace Medal. Bronze proof. Size 48. 1.50.

John Quincy Adams. Peace Medal. Br. proof. Size 48. 1.50.

Andrew Jackson. Peace Medal. Br. proof. Size 48. 1.50.

Same. Copper proof. Size 40. 1.00.

William H. Harrison. Bust to right ; rev., battle of the Thames. Bronze proof. Size 42. 1.50.

Zachary Taylor. For Palo Alto. Bronze proof. Size 40. 1.50.
Same. Rev., scene of battle of Buena Vista. Bronze proof. Size 57. 3.00.
View of the Battle of Buena Vista; rev., pelican feeding young. Presented to Gen.
 Taylor by Louisiana. Bronze proof. Size 48. 3.00.
Zachary Taylor. Peace Medal. Bronze proof. Size 48. 1.50.
Millard Fillmore. Bust to right, 1850; rev., Pioneer and Indian before an American
 flag. Bronze proof. Size 40. 1.50.
James Buchanan. "Embassy from Japan." Bronze proof. Size 48. 1.50.
Same. "To Frederick Rose, Ass't Surgeon U. S. Navy." Group of figures.
 Bronze proof, slightly stained on edge. Size 48. 1.50.
Abr. Lincoln. Rev., Indian plowing, scalping scene, etc. Bronze proof. Size 48.
 2.00.
Andrew Johnson. Rev., draped female with American flag grasping the hand of an
 Indian before a bust of Washington on a pedestal. Bronze proof. Size
 48. 1.50.
Same as last, but silver proof. Weighs 6½ oz. Av. 10.00.
U. S. Grant. Bust, "The oceans united by railway, May 10, 1869;" rev., mountain
 scenery, train of cars, etc. Silver proof. Size 28. Morocco case. 3.00.

Miscellaneous American Medals.

John Egar Howard. For battle of Cowpens. Bronze proof. Size 29. 1.00.
Wm. Washington, same battle, bronze proof, size 29. 1.00.
"Light-horse Harry" Lee, for battle of Paulus Hook, N. J., 1779. Silver. Dull
 proof. Size 29. 3.50.
Col. Geo. Crogan. Defense of Fort Stephenson, 1813; rev., view of the battle.
 Bronze proof. Size 40. 1.50.
Gov. Isaac Shelby, for battle of Thames, 1813; rev., view of the battle. Bronze
 proof. Size 40. 1.50.
Maj.-Gen'l. Alexander Macomb; rev., view of battle of Plattsburgh. Bronze proof.
 Size 40. 1.50.
Maj.-Gen'l. Winfield Scott; rev., beautiful views of seven battles. Bronze proof.
 Size 56. 3.00.
Maj.-Gen'l. Winfield Scott; bust on square tablet, "The Commonwealth of Virginia,"
 etc. Rev., column bearing names of battles in wreath. Bronze proof.
 Size 56. 3.00.
Maj.-Gen'l. Winfield Scott, for battle of Chippewa. Bronze proof. Size 40. 1.50.
Thos. Truxton; rev., scene of naval victory. Bronze proof. Size 36. 1.50.
Capt. James Biddle, capture of Penguin, 1815; rev., naval battle. Bronze proof.
 Size 40. 1.50.
Capt. Johnston Blakely, capture of Reindeer; rev., naval battle. Bronze proof. Size
 40. 1.50.
John Paul Jones. For victories off Scottish coast; rev., naval scene. Bronze proof.
 Size 36. 1.00.
Franklin; by Dupre; rev., "Eripuit Coelo," etc., in wreath. Bronze proof. Size 29.
 1.25.
Franklin; rev., angel, br. proof, size 29. 1.25.
Franklin, bust in fur cap; rev., Franklin Institute, Pa. Bronze proof. Size 24. 1.00.
Lafayette, by Cannois; rev., "Appele parte volu unanime, etc." Silver. Dull proof.
 Size 32. Weight 2½ oz. Av. 5.00.
Lafayette, by Cannois; rev., "The defender," etc. Bronze proof. Size 30. 1.25.
Henry Clay; rev., hand on rock, inscribed "Constitution." Bronze proof. Size 48.
 3.00.
Charles Carroll of Carrollton, by Gobrecht, on his 90th year; bronze proof; size 32.
 3.00.
Wreck of Steamer Metis; rev., life-saving scene. Bronze proof. Size 40. 2.50.
Rescue of crew of U. S. Brig Somers, 1846; scene of wreck; rev., scene of rescue.
 Bronze proof. Size 36. 2.00.

Humane Society of Massachusetts, 1866; shield with ship and boats, surmounted by
house of refuge. Bronze proof. Size 36. 2.00.
Tayleur medal, "Fund for shipwrecked strangers," view of shipwreck. Bronze
proof. Size 28. Rare. 2.00.
Sanitary Fair, Philadelphia, 1864, sick soldier, etc. Bronze proof. Size 36. 1.50.
Dr. Elisha Kane, bust above Arctic scene; rev., Masonic emblems. Bronze proof.
Size 32. 1.25.
Agassiz, bust to right. Bronze proof. Size 29. 1.25.
Washington Irving; rev,, date of birth. Bronze proof. Size 44. 3.50.
A. Thiers, from Philadelphia, 1873. Bronze proof. Size 29. 1.25.
Cyrus W. Field, for Atlantic Cable. Bronze proof. Size 32. 1.00.
Same. White metal proof. .25.
"Stonewall" Jackson, in japanned case, with glass to show each side. W. m. proof,
size with case 56. .50.
Quinnipiack medal, minister preaching, 1638; rev., view of New Haven, etc. Very
fine. Size 36. 2.00.
California State Agri. Soc. Award medal. Handsome landscape scene with ani-
mals including a large bear, fruits, etc. Very fine. Size 28. Weight 1½
oz. Av. 2.00.
1849. Salem Charitable Mech. Assoc. Hercules has just killed a winged dragon;
boys picking apples from an impossible tree. Size 28. Bronze proof. 1.25.

Centennial Medals.

The Centennial Award Medal, that granted to exhibitors. Seated female holding
olive branch, four smaller designs and 38 stars surrounding; rev., "Awarded
by Centennial Commission." As these award medals are highly prized by
the few who received them, scarcely any have been sold, and they are extremely rare. Size 48. In velvet-lined morocco case. 10.00.
Centennial Commission Medal. Size 36. Brass proof. .50.
Same. Smaller, size 24. Silver proof. 1.25.
Same as last, brass proof in case. .40.
Independence Hall: legend, "Proclame Liberty, etc.;" rev., Memorial Hall, "To
commemorate," etc. Bronze proof, size 37, in case. The handsomest U.
S. Centennial Medal. 2.00.
French Centennial. Beautiful head of Liberty; rev., crossed flags. Beautiful, ex-
ceeds anything issued in U. S. Bronze proof. Size 32. 2.50.
Brazilian Centennial. Dom Pedro II. (The king that has been lately overthrown).
" Exposicao Internaceonal de Philadelphia, 1876." Very fine and rare. 1.50.
Centennial. Wooden Medals. Oblong. 2¾x4 inches. Set of the five different
buildings 1.00.

Assay Medals.

1861. Head of Liberty. Br. proof. Size 21. 1.25.
1888. Grover Cleveland. Br. proof. Size 48. In handsome morocco velvet-lined
case. The largest of the Assay Medals. 5.00.
1889. Same as last, except date. In handsome velvet-lined wooden case. 5.00.

Foreign Medals.

(All bronze and perfect unless otherwise stated. Size given in sixteenths of an inch.)

Lord Byron, rev., poetic muse lamenting by the sea. 35. 2.50.
Flaxman, rev., Mercury carrying a muse. 36. 2.50.
Hogarth, rev., group of three male figures, 1848. 35. 2.50.
Wellington; rev., Vota Publica in wreath. 34. 1.50.
Wellington. 1815; rev., Minerva gives sword to Mars. 32. 2.00.
Lord Bacon, bust nearly facing; rev., Learning with starry robe flying over world.
Silver proof. 27. 4.00.
I. uis XVI., bust to right; rev., large bust of Queen to left, by Duvivier 1781, a.
beautiful medal. 47. 2.50.
N poleon, rev., copy of star of legion of honor. Beautiful. 26. 2.00.

Napoleon, bust in cocked hat; rev., urn and sword, etc., funeral medal, 1840, by
Roget, **very** beautiful. 33. 2.50.
Napoleon; rev's., **Fabius** Cunctator, orphan of Legion of Honor, Egyptian eagle, the
Alps. etc. **Silver** proof or nearly proof Size 25 Weight about 1¾ oz.
Av. each. 7 pcs. Lot 20.00.
Louis Philippe; rev., France offering the crown, Aug. 9, 1830. Beautiful. 48.
3.50.
Louis Philippe, busts of king and queen in separate medallions facing; rev., medal-
lions with heads of the whole royal family surrounded with allegorical fig-
ures. A magnificent medal, exquisitely designed. 50. 3.50.
Napoleon III. Rev., Empress. By Montagny. 34. 2.00.
Rubens. Bust almost facing in large hat, an exquisite piece of workmanship by
Hart. 1840. Rev., his monument at Antwerp. Very rare. 46. 5.00.
Sandwich Islands. Award medal of Hawaian Society, beautiful obverse. 40.
2.00.
Poland. Magnificent bust of **Augustus II.** with draped armor and laurel wreath.
Rev., Hercules supporting the Polish world, both sides in extremely high
relief. A beautiful work of very light olive bronze. 45. 5.00.
Series of Roman Historical Tokens. Busts of Romulus, Numa Pompilius and other
distinguished rulers to Augustus, also of orators, poets, etc., views of land
and sea battles, etc., etc., all with explanatory inscriptions. *No duplicates.*
Very rare series published at Paris by J. Dassier & Son. Only set in
America. Silver. Size 20. Finest possible condition. 60 pcs. 50.00.
Medallion plaques. Ebonized wood. 4⅜ inches in diameter, busts highly polished.
Queen Victoria and Prince Albert; Albert Edward, Prince of Wales, and
Alexandra, Princess; Napoleon III. and Eugenie; Napoleon I. and Victor
Emmanuel II. 8 pcs. Lot for 5.00.
Wagner. Fine portrait by Wiener. Rev., characters representing his different
operas grouped on bridge inscribed BAYREUTH. Beautifully designed and
executed. Bronze proof. Size 45. 5.00.
England. William IV. 1830. A superb frosted silver medal by Chantry, sur-
rounded by projecting silver band to protect medal. Bust to right; rev.,
" Adelaide regina cudi jussit, 1830," in wreath with trident. Extremely
fine. Excessively rare. Weight 5 oz. Size 44. 12.50.
Sweden. Gustavus Adolphus. Mortuary medal. 1634. Recumbent figure of the
King, crowned and in armor, cherubs on clouds above, pursuing and flee-
ing troops in the distance, inscription on border and in exergue. Rev.,
the King, crowned by Religion and Victory in triumphing chariot drawn
drawn by winged horses passes over prostrate foes and hydra, ET VITA
ET MORTE TRIUMPHO above, inscription on border. Superb and
rare silver medal, in brilliant, almost proof condition. Size 50. 50.00.

Masonic Medals.

Hopkins Lodge. Black Jack Grove, Texas. Silver, brass and copper proofs. Size
14. Lot 1.00.
Lake City Lodge, Florida, No. 27. Marvin 290. Brass proof. Size 18. .35.
St. Albans, Phil'a, No. 47. Shield shaped Centennial. Tin. Size 24x32. .25.
Solomon's Lodge, No. 1. Po'keepsie, N. Y. Head of Washington. Copper and
brass proofs. Size 22. Pair. 75.
"Hollandsche Loge Staat Van Nieuw York, 5787." Copper proof. Size 20. .50.
Hermit Commandery, No. 24, Lebanon, Pa. Beautiful nine-pointed bronze medal
(size 34) in the centre of which is handsome relief design of cave, knight
greeting hermit. Mounted on the ribbon are also triangle (size 25) with
name of commandery and small oval with " 24." 5.00.
Mary Commandery, No. 36, Phil'a. Shield-shaped badge with design of Christ and
Mary, " Rabboni" below. Rev., inscription. Tin. Size 23x36. 1.00.
Mary Commandery. Masonic Cross, " Mary-1869-1876." Bronze. Size 24. 1.00.
Cyrene Commandery, Camden, N. J. Relief on solid background showing cross-

bearer and crossed swords.   Finely designed.   Brass and tin.   Size 20. Pair 2.00.

Triennial Conclave, San Francisco.   Knight on horseback.   Gold.   Size 8.   1.00.

Phil'a Commandery's Pilgrimage to San Francisco.   Brass proof.   Size 20.   Marvin 84.   .35.

Triennial Conclave, Chicago, 1880.   Masonic Cross (size 24) with pin and ribbon. Tin.   1.00.

"Du Point Parfait A L'o—De Paris."   Marvin 164.   Bronze.   About proof.   Size 18.   .75.

Egyptain Obelisk.   Marvin 712.   Silver proof.   Size 22.   1.50.

Same.   Bronze proof.   .75

Philadelphia Commandery, No. 2.   Bell-shaped Centennial.   Silvered.   Perfect. Size 32x32.   .50.

Olive Branch, No. 39, N. Y.   W. metal proof.   Size 26.   .25.

Kadosh Commandery, No. 23, Phila.   W. metal, proof, size 29.   .35.

Miscellaneous Cards, etc.

1822 Dime counterstamped with heads of Lafayette and Washington in procession, 1824 (reception of Lafayette).   2.50.

1820 Cent, similar counterstamp, the best impression of these counterstamps I have seen.   2.50.

Beck's Public Baths.   Female washing her feet.   Rare card.   Very good.   1.50.

1837.   Card of Nathan C. Folger, New Orleans.   Brass.   Size 22.   Very fine. One in the Levick sale bought $11.25.   3.50.

10 cents.   Encased postage stamp.   2.00.

5 cents.   Encased postage stamp.   Bailey & Co., Phil'a.   1.50.

3 cents.   Encased postage stamp.   Drake's Bitters.   1.25.

Am I not a Woman and a Sister ?   Negress in chains.   Very fine.   .50.

Am I not a Man and a Brother?   Negro in chains.   Size 21.   Tin.   Good.   1.00.

Same design, cameo, negro in black.   Oval.   Size 17x20.   Very fine.   2.00.

Lee and Reynolds, Cheyenne Agency.   Nickle card.   Size 20.   Buffalo on obverse. Fine and rare.   1.00.

First Steam Coinage at U. S. Mint, Mar. 23, 1836.   Cap in rays.   Bronze proof. Size 18.   .25.

Same but dated Feb 22, 1836.   Very good.   Rare.   .50.

John Brown, "Slavery the sum of all villainies ; " rev., Brown hanging, 1859.   W. m. proof.   Size 20.   1.00.

"No submission to the North," 1860.   Palmetto tree, cannon, etc.   Rev., " The Wealth of the South," rice, tobacco, sugar, cotton.   Copper, brass and tin. Also, reverse muled with shield, tin and brass, and with John Bell in copper.   6 pieces.   Perfect.   Rare lot.   3.00.

Jeff Davis hanging; rev., "Death to traitors."   Brass token.   Uncirculated.   1.00.

Swedish Plate Money.

Two Dalers.   Frederick.   Counterstamped F. R. S. 1743 crowned in each corner. 2 DALER SILF MYNT in centre.   Very fine.   Measures 7x7¾ inches. 12.50.

One Daler.   1745.   Same design.   Very fine.   7.50.

Copper Coins and Medals of British America.

1674.   Bust of Louis XIV., in flowing hair.   Rev., emblematic of victory over the Dutch at Martinque.   Bronze proof.   Size 26.   2.50.

1886.   Brantford, Ont., Thayendanagea : fine bust of the chief; rev., his monument. Bronze proof.   Size 24.   1.50.

Halifax Ferry Token.   Steamboat.   Uncirculated.   Bright red, proof.   2.00.

White' Farthing, Halifax.   Very fine.   5.00.

Starr and Shannon.   Indian and dog.   Extremely fine.   Light olive.   .75.

Francis Mullins & Son.   Very fine.   1.00.

Robert Purvis. Uncirculated. .75.
H. Gagnon. Beaver. Uncirculated. 1.25.
T. S. Brown & Co. Fine. Brown. .35.
J. Shaw & Co. Very fine. Olive. .50.
J. Brown. Fine. Brown. .35.
Carriett & Alport. Very fine. Olive. .50.
Miles W. White. Very good. .35.
John Alexander. Very good. .25.
Hostermann & Etter. 1814. Fine. .50.
Same. 1815. Smaller. Fine. .35.
Lesslie & Sons. Half-penny. Fine. .25.
" No labour, no bread." Very fine. Olive. .50.
Magdalen Island. Seal and dried codfish. Fine. 1.50.
Montreal and Lachine Railroad Co. Engine and beaver. Large. Extra fine.
     3.00.
Montreal. " De L'isle de Montreal a Repentigny on Lachesnaye." "Charette"
     token. Fine. Very rare. 10.00.
Nova Scotia and New Brunswick. Ship, "Success" below. About uncirculated.
     Light olive. 5.00.
Ships, Colonies and Commerce. Rev., harp. As usually found. Unknown to Le-
     Roux. 5.00.

Continental and Colonial Notes, Badges, Etc.

Continental. 1778. April 11. $4. Yorktown. Very fine. 5.00.
1778. April 11. $5. Yorktown. Fine. 5.00.
1778. April 11. $6. Yorktown. Fine. 5.00.
1778. April 11. $7. Yorktown. Very fine. 5.00.
1778. April 11. $30. Yorktown. Very fine. 5.00.
Vermont. 1781. Feb., 2s. 6d. Fine and excessively rare. 35.00.
Massachusetts. Jan. 22, 1777. £10. An extremely large and very rare note.
     6¾x7¾ inches. Very fine. Signed by W. Cooper and N. Appleton.
     7.50.
Delaware. 1758. May. 1. 20sh. Printed by Ben Franklin. Lion on reverse.
     Very good. 1.00.
North Carolina. 1776. April 2, $10. Peacock. Good. .75.
1778. $5, 10, 20. Good. Lot. 1.50.
Georgia. 1777. Oct. 16. 1sh, 2sh. 6d, 5, 10, 20sh. Long notes. Hand hold-
     ing Constitution. Uncirculated. Lot. 12.50.
1778. $30. Blue hog. Very fine. 5.00.
1778. $40. Hand holding dagger and dove. Very fine. 5.00.
Hungarian Independence. Louis Kossuth. Feb. 2, 1852. $1. Uncirculated. 1.00.
Badges. Harrison. Campaign of 1840. Portrait of Harrison, typical figures,
     eagle, owl and beaver above, " Tippecanoe and Fort Meigs" below. 1.50.
Henry Clay. Portrait. Indian with shield above. .50.
Lafayette. Old, 1824 probably. 1.00.
Washington. Centennial Celebration, 1832. .50.
American Manufactures and Ireland's Independence Solidarity with attached medal,
     size 24, " We purpose 'fore high heaven till Erin's chains are riven," etc.
     .50.

Fractional Currency.

(All new and clean.)

50, 25, 10, 5 Cents. Perforated edges. 5.00.
50, 25, 10, 5 Cents. Plain edges. 2.00.
50, 25, 10, 5 Cents. Washington in gilt ring. 2.50.
50, 25, 10, 5 Cents. Washington in gilt ring. Paper that will split. 5.00.
50 Cents. Justice. Red back. Auto. sign. of Colby and Spinner. Coarse fibre
     paper. 5.00.

50 Cents. Justice. Red back. Auto. sign. of Colby and Spinner. Plain paper.
    3.50.
50 Cents. Justice. Red back. No letters on rev. 2.50.
50 Cents. Justice. Green back. Coarse fibre paper. 3.50.
50 Cents. Justice. Green back. 2.00.
50 Cents. Spinner. Red back. Auto. sign. of Colby and Spinner. 3.50.
50 Cents. Spinner. Red back. 2.25.
50 Cents. Spinner. Green back. "50" at ends. 1.50.
50 Cents. Spinner. Green back. "50" in centre. 1.75.
25 Cents. Fessenden. Red back. 1.50. Green back. .50.
25 Cents. Fessenden. Green back. Coarse fiber paper, gilt letters on reverse.
    Heavy but not solid disc. 5.00.
25 Cents. Fessenden. Green back. Coarse fiber paper. Solid discs. 20.00.
15 Cents. Grant and Sherman. Red back. Auto. sign. of Allison and Spinner. 8.00
15 Cents. Grant and Sherman. Green back. Auto. sign. of Jeffries and Spinner.
    6.00.
10 Cents. Washington. Red back. Auto. sign. of Colby and Spinner. 1.50.
10 Cents. Washington. Red back. 1.00. Green back. .35.
 5 Cents. Clark. Red back. .75. Green back. .35.
 3 Cents. Washington. .40. Dark curtain. .75.
50 Cents. Lincoln. 1.50.
50 Cents. Stanton. .85.
25 Cents. Washington. .50.
15 Cents. Liberty. .60.
10 Cents. Liberty. .35.
50 Cents. Crawford. .75.
50 Cents. Dexter. .75.
50 Cents. Crawford. Auto. sign. of "Jno. C. New." 5.00.
25 Cents. Walker. .50.
10 Cents. Merideth. Green seal. .50. Red seal. .25.
Shield of Fractional Currency as issued by U. S. Contains two Grant and Sherman
    15 cent notes, etc. 15.00.

The following are all extremely rare.

50 Cents. 2nd issue. No gilt ring around Washington. Coarse fiber paper. Plain
    reverse. 7.50.
50 Cents. 2nd issue. The obverse has the large gilt outline 50 and gilt figures in
    corners usually found on the reverse, otherwise plain. The reverse is the
    usual design, but with the gilt ring usually found on the obverse around the
    50, and lacking the designs which on this note are on the obverse. Coarse
    fiber paper. 7.50.
50 Cents. 2nd issue. Obverse plain except a gilt ring; reverse as usual. Coarse
    fiber paper. 7.50.
10 Cents. 2nd issue. Obverse plain except a gilt ring; reverse as usual. Coarse
    fiber paper. 7.50.
 5 Cents. 2nd issue. Obverse plain; reverse lacks the outlined figure and is differ-
    ently shaded from the regular note, the eagle and stars on border being light
    where dark on the usual note and *vice versa*. The color is a light gold-
    brown. *Unique.* 15.00.

Hard Times Tokens.

Negress in chains. "Am I not a woman and a sister?" Very good. .25.
Steer. "A friend to the Constitution." Rev., ship, "Agriculture and Commerce."
    Very good. .75.
Donkey. Rev., turtle. Uncirculated. Bright red. .25.
Loco Foco. Uncirculated. Bright and olive. One of best I have seen. 1.25.
Head of Jackson; rev., hog running. Uncirculated. Partly bright. .40.
Same. *Brass.* Uncirculated. 2.00.
Jackson in safe; rev., ship. Uncirculated. Beautiful purple color. .75.

Ship; rev., wrecked ship. Uncirculated. Purple and bright. .40.
1837. Liberty head. 13 stars. No. 27. Very good. 1.00.
1837. Liberty head. 15 stars (a small star on each side of date). No. 28. Very good. 1.00.
1837. "United" head, large date. No. 29. Good. 1.00.

Ancient and Foreign Gold.

Turkey. Gold. Proof. Size 14. 2.00.
Transylvania. 1657. George Rakoczi II. Ducat. Uncirculated. 6.00.
Salzburg. 1714. Francis Anton. ¼ Ducat. Uncirculated. 2.00.
Nordlingen. 1497. Ducat. The 4 in loop form. One of the earliest dated coins. Very fine. 7.50.
Nurnberg. Two pretty little gold coins with lamb and standard. The smallest is only 7 cts. in gold. Uncirculated. Pair 3.00.
Guatemala. 1860. 4 Reals. Uncirculated. 1.25.
New Grenada. 1837. Dollar. About uncirculated. 1.75.
Honduras. 1846. Dollar. Mountain peaks. Uncirculated. 1.75.
Mexico. 1826–1828–1862. Dollars. About uncirculated. Lot 5.00.
Spain. 1788. Dollar. About uncirculated. 1.75.
Papal States. 1853. Scudo. Semi-proof. 2.00.
France. Nap. III. 1854. 5 Francs. Uncirculated. 1.75.
India. 1–128 Mohur. Extremely small. Uncirculated. 1.50.
Japan. ¼ Koban. Oval. ⅞x1½ in. About uncirculated. 3.50.
England. 1803. Geo. III. ½ Guinea. *Brilliant proof.* 7.50.
England. 1797. Geo. III. 1/3 Guinea. Uncirculated. Brilliant mint bloom. 5.00.
England. 1718. Geo. I. ¼ Guinea. Uncirculated. Brilliant mint bloom. 6.00.
Japan. Oblong. ¼, ½, 1 Bou. Latter ¾ inch long. Lot 3.50.
Russia. 3 Roubles. Platinum. About uncirculated. 4.00.
Olmuntz. Wolfgang. ¼ Ducat. Very fine. 1.75.
Roman. (457) Leo I. Rev., Victory holding a cross. Solidus. Very good. 5.00.
(474) Zeno. Rev., Victory holding a cross. Solidus. Very good. 5.00.
(630) Heraclius and son. Rev., cross on pedestal. Solidus. Very fine. 6.00.

Oriental Silver.

Anam. Taele or Dragon Dollar. Grinning human-faced dragon's head above sun; rev., 4 characters around sun. Uncirculated. Rare. 5.00.
Anam. Silver duk. Dragons. Extremely fine. 2.00.
Bidsnagur, India. Half Fanam. Dancing deity. Very fine. 1.00.
Madras. Quarter Pagoda. Tower surrounded by stars; rev., god Vishnu in circle of dots. Fine. 1.50.
Assam. Octagonal Rupee. Very fine. Rare. 2.00.
Burmah. Rupee, ⅛ and 1–16. Peacock with spread tail. Very fine. Lot 3.00.
Japan. Itzebue. Uncirculated. .75.
Japan. ¼ Itzebue. Uncirculated. .35.
Siam. Bullet money. Tical. Very fine. 1.25.
Siam. Bullet money. ¼ and ⅛ Tical. Very fine. Each .75.
Persia. ¼ Kran. Sun-lion with sword (dime size). Uncirculated. .50.
Persia. Kran. Sun-lion. Uncirculated. 1.00.
Japan. Oblong silver coin, 3½x1⅜ in. The obverse is covered with characters, also two circular stamps with characters near each end. Fine and rare. Weight 4½ oz. Av. 10.00.
Japan. Oblong, one pear shaped, silver dumps, each stamped with characters. They range in size from a pea to ¾ oz. I do not think two sizes are alike. Fine lot. 13 pieces. 12.50.
Siam. Circulars coin with elephant and royal umbrellas. 2, 1, ⅛ Tical. About uncirculated. 5.00.
Corea. 1 and 2 Stubs (size 14 and 18.) Coined as indemnity money to China. Obverse with porcelain centre; rev., four characters. Very curious and rare. Uncirculated. Pair for 5.00.

Cambodia.   Bird idol.   Very fine.   Size 8.   .50.
Saurashtran, Hindu.   Curious figure somewhat resembling a pelican.   Size 10.
    Fine.   1.50.
India.   Small dump with idol.   Fine.   .50.
Morocco.   1284.   Size 12.   Very good.   .40.
Java.   1802.   Ship.   1–16, ⅛, ¼, ½, 1 Gulden.   Uncirculated.   Rare set.   7.50.
Java.   1801 and 1805.   Rupees, large and small.   Zoerabaya mint.   Good and un-
    circulated.   Pair 2.50.
China.   Spanish Dollar covered with Chinese chop-marks, a number of which are
    die-stamps of various designs.   2.50.
India.   Travancore.   Small dumps with idols.   Two sizes.   Very fine.   Pair 1.00.
Georgia.   Rupee and half.   Extremely fine and uncirculated.   Pair 1.50.
Cambodia.   Tical.   Odd-looking bird.   Rev., turreted temple.   Uncirculated.   5.00.
Siam.   Head of King.   Rev., arms with four elephants.   Franc size.   Uncirculated.
    1.25.
Madras.   1, 2, 5 Fanam.   About uncirculated.   Lot 1.50.
Madras.   Half and Quarter Pagoda.   Tower surrounded by stars; rev., God Vishnu
    in circle of dots.   Value in four languages.   Uncirculated.   Beautiful pair.
    6.00.
Anam.   Similar in design to Chinese cash with square hole in centre.   Size 20.
    Uncirculated.   Rare.   5.00.
Sandwich Islands.   Dime.   1883.   Uncirculated.   .35.
Mauritius.   1886.   10 Cents.   Uncirculated.   .35.

Foreign Silver.

New Grenada.   1849.   Head of Liberty.   Pattern Peso by Wyon.   4 designs
    Beautiful proofs.   Lot for 10.00.
Sweden.   1871.   Chas. XV.   4 R. M., 2 R. M., 50, 25, 10 Ore.   *Beautiful proofs.*
    Set for 5.00.
Central America.   Dollar.   Sun rising behind mountain peaks.   But little circulated.
    Semi-proof.   1.50.
Republic of Columbia.   1820.   Dollar.   Indian head and pomegranate.   Excep-
    tionally fine for this piece.   2.00.
U. S. of Colombia.   1868.   Half Dollar.   Very fine.   1.00.
Bolivia.   1845.   Llamas under tree.   Dollar.   Uncirculated.   Mint lustre.   2.50.
Peru.   1833.   Liberty standing.   Dollar.   Barely circulated.   Mint lustre.   2.00.
Peru.   1862, 1863, 1864.   Callao and Lima.   Indian, Liberty in chariot, steamboat.
    Tokens.   ¼ dollar size.   Semi-proof.   3 pieces.   Lot.   2.50.
Chili.   1874.   Dollar.   Condor.   Barely circulated.   1.50.
Chili.   Mining Dollar.   Plain planchet with star and 1 P. in sunken counterstamp.
    Fine.   2.00.
La Plata.   1, 2, 4, 8 Reals (Dollar).   Sun in Rays.   Very fine.   Lot.   3.00.
Cordoba.   (Argentine onf.)   C Dollar.   Fort surrounded by seven flags.   Very fine.
    Rare.   5.00.

Venezuela. 1858. Half Dollar. Fine. 1.00.
Ecuador. 1855. Half Dollar. Fine. 1.00.
Caracas. 1811. 2 Reals. Very fine. Rude. .40.
France. Louis XIIII. 1653. Crown. Young head. Very fine. 2.50.
Bavaria. Maximilian II. 1853. ½, 1, 2 Gulden, 1 Thaler. Uncirculated. Mint
  bloom. Lot 2.50.
Neapolitan Republic. Liberty standing. Year 7. Fine. 2.50.
Russia. 1860. Rouble. Proof. 1.00.
Sicily. 1855. Ferd. II. Crown. Uncirculated. 1.25.
Sandwich Islands. Kalakaua I. Dime. Brilliant proof. .50.
Japan. Dragon. Yen, 50, 20, 10, 5 sen. Uncirculated. Lot 2.50.
Bolivia. 1868. Pattern set. 5, 10, 20 Centavos, 1 Boliviano. State Arms. Rev.,
  Condor standing. Silver proofs. 7.50.
Bolivia. 1884. 5, 10, 20, 50 Centavos, 1 Boliviano. State Arms. Brilliant proofs
  7.50.
Sierra Leone. 1791. Dollar. Lion. Sharp, uncirculated, proof surface. 7.50.
Hayti. 1881. Gourde (Dollar), 20, 10 cts. Beautiful design. Brilliant mint
  lustre. Set 2.50.
Switzerland. 1814. Canton Soloth'n. Crown. Fine. 2.00.
New Grenada. 1847. 2, 8 Reals. Very fine Scarce. Pair 1.50.
Bolivia. 1884. Dime. Br. Proof. .50.
Sardinia. 1859. Victor Emmanuel. 5 Lire. Brilliant mint lustre. 1.50.
Papal States. 1836. Gregory XVI. Scudo. Uncir'd. 1.50.
Austria. 1780. Maria Theresa. Levant Crown. Uncir'd. 1.50.
Brunswick. 1670, etc. Wild man. 4, 6, 12, 24 Gros. Very fine. Lot 2.50.
Mexico. 1866. Maxmilian. Dollar and half. Barely circulated. Pair 2.50.
1841. Bolivia. Bolivar. Llamas under tree. Dollar. Barely cir'd. 1.50.
1842. Peru. Dollar. Liberty with spear and shield. Very fine. Mint lustre.
  1.50.
1867. Peru. Dollar. Seated Liberty. Uncirculated. 1.25.
1877. Chili. Dollar. Condor. Uncirculated. 1.50.
Japan. Dollar. Dragon and sun. Uncirculated. 1.50.
1821. Spain. Ferd. VII. Dollar. About uncirculated. 1.25.
1817. Spain. Ferd. VII. Dollar. Counterstamped for Brazil. Extremely fine.
  1.25.
Tranquebar. Dump with idol. Very fine. .65.
France. Napoleon III. 1852. ½, 1 fr. Uncirculated. 2 pcs. Lot. .50.
India. Old rupee, curious die-counterstamp of man on horseback. Very fine. 2.00.
Assam. Octagonal rupee, curious dragon at bottom, extremely fine. 2.00.
Kempten. Bust of the Bishop. Bracteates. Size 14. Uncirculated. 10 pcs. Lot
  2.50.
Lille. Marshal's batons crowned, rev., mailed arm with sword. "Non sine
  numine," necessity money, very fine, size 19. 1.50.
Small bracteates. 25 pcs. Lot. 1.00.
Mexico. 1812. Vargas dollar. Fair (never found better). 1.25.
Central America. Sun rising behind mountain peaks. 1, 2 reals. Pair. .50.
Guatemala. 1808. Ferd. VII. Proclamation 1, 2 reals. Mountain. Very good.
  Pair. 2.00.
Same. 1 real. Good. Pierced. .35.
Guatemala. Sept. 24, 1812. 2 reals. Open book in rays, arms of Guatemala.
  Fine. Pierced. .50.
Louis XV. and XVI. Tokens. 1735, 1741, etc. ½, ¼ (3) Crowns. Ship under
  full sail, Justice with scales, tree growing, etc. Fine. 4 pcs. 2.50.
Republic. 1849. 20, 50c., 1, 5 Francs. Uncirculated. Mint bloom. Lot. 1.75.
Republic. 1852. Louis Napoleon Bonaparte. 50c., 1, 5 Francs. Uncirculated.
  Mint bloom. 1.75.
Chili. 1817. Dollar. Volcano ; rev., pillar surmounted by globe. Barely circu-
  lated. Lustre. 2.00.

Prussia. 1871. Siege Thaler. Uncirculated. Mint bloom. 2.50.
Berne. 1795. Dollar. Swiss soldier. Rev., Bear on shield. *Proof.* A beauty.
          5.00.
Canton Zurich. 1813. Dollar. Semi-proof. A beauty. 5.00.
Canton Luzerne. 1814. Dollar. Swiss soldier. *Proof.* A beauty. 5.00.
Persia. Sun-lion with sword. 2 Francs. Uncirculated. 1.00.
Chili. 1839. Dollar. Condor breaking chains. Barely circulated. 1.50.
Peru. 1822. Dollar. Coat of arms with flags; rev., Justice and Liberty standing
          beside column. Fine and rare. 2.00.
France. 1844. Louis Philippe. 5 Francs. Br. proof. 2.50.
1789. Louis XVI. Crown. About uncirculated. 3.00.

Silver Coins of Great Britain.

Early British. Cunobeline. Head to right. Rev., Pegasus on dotted base. Gold
          ¼ Stater. Extremely fine. 7.50.
Early British Tetradrachm. Idiotic head; rev., shadowy horseman on colossal
          horse. Very fine. 6.00.
Stycae. Rude horse. Copper. Fine. 1.50.
Ethelred II. 978. Holding sceptre, large cross on rev. Silver penny. Very
          fine. 2.00.
Ethelred II. 978. Copper Styca. Extremely fine. 1.25.
Canute. 1017. Silver penny. Fine. 2.00.
Edward the Confessor. 1042. Silver penny. Bust with sceptre. SWETHAN
          ON LYN. Extremely fine. 3.00.
Another. King enthroned. Chichester mint. Very fine. 3.00.
William the Conqueror. 1066. Silver penny. Fine. 2.00. Good. 1.50.
Henry II. 1154. Silver penny. Good. 1.00.
Richard I. 1189. Pictaine silver penny. Very good. 1.50.
Henry III. 1216. Silver penny. Very good. .50.
Edward I. 1272. Silver penny. Fine. .50.
Edward I. 1272. Groat. Good. .75.
Edward II. 1307. Silver penny. Very fine. 1.25.
Edward III. 1327. Groat. Very fine. 1.50.
Henry V. 1413. Groat. Very fine. 1.50.
Henry VI. 1422. Groat. Very fine. 1.00.
Edward IV. 1461. Groat. Good. .75.
Edward IV. 1461. Halfpenny. Very good. .75.
Henry VII. 1485. Groat. Front face. Fine. 1.25.
Henry VII. 1485. Groat. Side view. Extremely fine. 2.00.
Henry VII. 1485. Half Groat. Issued by Archbishop Morton. Good. 1.50.
Henry VIII. 1509. Groat. Side view. Fine. .75.
Henry VIII. 1509. Groat. Front face. Fine. 1.00. Good. .50.
Henry VIII. 1509. Silver penny. Very fine. 1.50.
Edward VI. 1547. Groat. Good. .75.
Edward VI. 1547. Broad Shilling. Very fine. 2.00. Fine. 1.50.
Mary. 1553. Groat. Very fine. 2.00. Good. 1.25.
Mary. 1553. Groat. Bust of Mary. Legend " Philip and Maria." Fine. 2.00.
Elizabeth. 1601. Crown. Very good, fine for this piece. Very rare. 20.00.
Elizabeth. 1558. Shilling. Very good. .75.
Elizabeth. 1562. Milled Sixpence. Extremely fine. 2.00.
Elizabeth. 1602. Hammered Sixpence. Very fine. .75.
James I. 1603. Half Crown. King on horseback. Very fair. 1.25.
James I. 1603. Shilling. Fine. 1.25. Very good. .75.
James I. 1605. Sixpence. Fine. .75. Good. .50.
Charles I. 1625. Half Crown. Portcullis. Very fine. 7.50.
Charles I. 1625. Half Crown. Briot's. Very fine. 7.50.
Charles I. 1625. Half Crown. King on horseback. Good. 2.00.
Charles I. 1625. Shilling. But little circulated. 4.00.

Charles I. 1625. Shilling. Fine. .75. Good. .50.
Charles I. Threepence, Welsh. Halfpenny. Rose. Very fine. Pair. 1.50.
Charles I. 1625. Ormond Crown, Half Crown, Shilling and Sixpence. Good.
    Set for 20.00.
Commonwealth. 1653. Half Crown. About uncirculated. 12.50.
Commonwealth. 1653. Twopence. Fine. 1.00.
Commonwealth. 1653. Penny. Fine. 1.00. Good. .75.
Commonwealth. 1653. Halfpenny. Fine. Rare. 1.50.
Oliver Cromwell. 1658. Crown. A beautiful uncirculated specimen, the crack in
    the die scarcely showing. 50.00.
Oliver Cromwell. 1658. Crown. Only the barest touch of circulation on most
    prominent parts of obverse. 30.00. Another, fine. 20.00.
Oliver Cromwell. 1658. Half Crown. Brilliant proof. Said to be the finest
    known. 75.00.
Oliver Cromwell. 1658. Half Crown. Extremely fine. 20.00. Very good.
    10.00.
Oliver Cromwell. 1658. Shilling. Barely circulated. 15.00. Fine. 10.00.
Charles II. 1665. Pattern farthing in silver. Uncirculated. 3.50.
Charles II. Maundy Set. Milled. Uncirculated. 3.00.
James II. 1687. Crown. Uncirculated. Mint bloom. 15.00.
James II. 1687. 40 Shilling piece. Extremely fine. 7.50.
James II. Maundy Set. Extremely fine. 2.50.
William and Mary. 1690. Half Crown. Rev., crowned shield. Uncirculated.
    Mint bloom. 3.50.
William and Mary. 1693. Half Crown. Rev., 4 shields, monogram W M and
    date in angles. Very good. 1.50.
William and Mary. 1689. 3 and 4 pence. Very fine. Pair 1.00.
William III. 1698. Half Crown. Uncirculated, some proof surface. 4.00.
Anne. 1707. Crown. Rev., roses and plumes in the angles. Fine. 3.00.
George II. 1732. Half Crown. 1758. Shilling. 1741, 1757. Sixpences, vari-
    eties. Uncirculated. Lot 4.00.
George II. Maundy Set. 1730-1743. Uncirculated. 2.00.
George III. Northumberland Shilling. 1763. Proof. 7.50.
George III. 1787. Sixpence and Shilling. Uncirculated. Semi-proof. Pair 1.25.
1804. Bank of England. Dollar. Fine. 1.75.
George III. 1818. Pistrucci Crown. St. George and the dragon. Proof. 7.50.
George III. 1819. Pistrucci Crown. St. George and the dragon. Proof. 7.50.
George III. 1762-1784. Maundy Set. Proofs. 2.00.
George III. 1800. Maundy Set. Small head, large bust. Proofs except 3 pence
    which is 1795, uncirculated. 2.00.
George III. 1820. Maundy Set. Bull head. Proofs. 2.50.
George IV. 1823. Maundy Set. Proofs. 2.00.
William IV. 1830. Maundy Set. Proofs. 2.50.
Victoria. Gothic Crown. Smooth edge. Brilliant proof. 25.00.
Victoria. 1844-1872. Maundy Set. Uncirculated. 1.50.
Victoria. 1888. Maundy Set. Proofs. 2.50.
Scotland. Alexander III. 1249. Silver penny. Extremely fine. 2.50.
David II. 1329. Groat. Good. 1.00.
David II. 1329. Silver Penny. Crowned bust. Very fine. 2.00.
Robert II. 1370. Groat. Very good. 1.50.
Robert II. 1370. Silver penny. Very fine. 2.00.
James II. 1437. Silver penny. Thistle. Fine but part of legend off. .75.
Mary. Billion Plack. Thistle. Good. 1.50.
Mary. "Nonsunt." M. crowned. Rev., "I AM NON SVNT DVO SED VNA
    CARO." Good. 2.00.
James VI. 1594. Thistle Mark. Bust of James; rev., thistle. Fine. 5.00.
James VI. 1601. Thistle Mark. Shield; rev., thistle. Fine. 5.00.
Ireland. 1723. Wood Sixpence. Similar in design to the Wood halfpence, which

were rejected in Ireland and then extensively circulated in America.   Extremely fine and *excessively rare.* 25.00.

Edward I. 1272. Silver penny. Head in triangle. Struck for Ireland. Very fine. 1.50.

James I. Shilling. Bust; rev., harp. "Henricus Rosas Regna Jacobus." Very good. 2.00.

Foreign Coppers.

Where more than one piece is given on a line, the price s for all and not per piece.

Antigua. 1836. Palm tree. Farthing. Fine. .50.

Argentine Confederation. Head of Liberty. 1, 2 Centavos. Uncirculated. Bright red. .50.

Andora. 1873. 10 Centimes. Proof. The only coin of this little republic. .25.

Bolivia. 1883. 1, 2 Centavos. Proof. .50.

British Honduras. 1885. Cent. Uncirculated. Bright red. .25.

Barbadoes. Penny. Negro head and pineapple. Fine. .75. Good. .50.

Barbadoes. Penny and Halfpenny. Neptune in car. Also, Penny. Pineapple. Set of 3 pcs. Proofs. Handsome. 15.00.

Bermuda. 1793. Penny. Extremely fine. Light olive. .75.

Bahama. Halfpenny. Ship sailing. Uncirculated. Brown. .50.

Bulgaria. 1879–1887. 10 Centimes. Uncirculated. Set of 5 pieces. .50.

Byzantine (Constantinople before the Turkish occupation). Cup-shaped. Fine. 1.00 Good. .50.

Congo Free States. 1, 2, 5, 10 Centimes. Round hole in centre. Uncirculated. Bright red. Set for .35.

Cambodia. Norodom I. 1860. 5, 10 Centesimos. Beautiful proofs. .50.

Cyprus. 1, ½, ¼ Piastre. Uncirculated. Bright red. 1.00.

Ceylon. 1815. ½, 1, 2 Stivers. Elephant. Very good and fine. 2.00.

Carthagena. Indian under tree. ¼, 2 R. Very good. .75.

Cape of Good Hope. 1889. Penny. Brilliant proof. .50.

Caracas. ¼ R. Very fine. .25.

Dominica. 1848. ¼ R. Very fine. .25.

Dominica. 1877. Centavo. Uncirculated. .25.

Dominica. 1877. 2½ Centavos. Nickel. Proof. .25.

Dutch East Indies. 6 St. 4¾ inches long. VI—St at each end on both sides. Very fine. Excessively rare. 15.00.

England. 1675. Carolus A Carolo. Farthing. Fine. .50. Good. .25.
1714. Anne. Farthing. Bust; rev., Britannia seated, 1714. Uncirculated. Glossy
light brown color. 15.00.
Geo. III. 1797. Twopenny. Weight 2 oz. Uncirculated. 2.50. Fine. 1.50.
Good. 1.00. Fair. .50.
1797. Geo. III. Penny. Weight 1 oz. Uncirculated. 1.50.
1847. Victoria. ½ Farthing. Uncirculated. Bright red. .20.
1793. Coventry Halfpenny. Lady Godiva; rev., elephant. Fine. .75. Good. .50.
1794. Similar; rev., clock tower. Fine. .50.
1795. Similar; rev., elephant. Extremely rare. Not in Conder. Very fine. Light
brown. 5.00.
Ecuador. 1872. 1, 2 Centavos. Very good. Rare. 1.50.
Ecuador. 1884. ½, 1 Centavos. Nickel. Very rare. Very fine pair. 2.50.
France. Henry III. Double Tournois. Fine. .35.
Guatemala. 1871. Centavo. Mountain peaks. Good. .50.

Greece. Head. 1, 2, 5, 10 Lepta. Uncirculated. Bright red. 1.00.
Guiana (Spanish). Lion; rev., castle. Very good. Rude. .50.
Guernsey. 1, 2, 4, 8 Doubles. 1889. Uncirculated. Bright red. .50.
Griquatown (South Africa). 1890. Penny. Br. proof. .25.
Hayti. 1877. Mercury head. 20 Cent. Proof. .25.
Hong Kong. Cent and Mil. Uncirculated. Bright. .30.
Island of Sumatra. Fine. .25.
Ionian Isles. ¼, ½, 1, 2 Obolo. Fine set. 2.00.
Isle of Man. 1733. Eagle and cradle. This and the following have the three
legs joined on reverse. Very good. .50.
1786. George III. Penny and Halfpenny. Fine. .75.
1813. Head of Geo. III. Uncirculated. Light olive. 1.50. Nearly as choice. 1.00.
Island of Ceylon. Vidschaya Bahu II. 1186–1187. Same. Massa. Very fine. 1.00.
Bhuvanaika Bahu. 1296–1314. Same. Massa. Very fine. 1.00.
Ireland. Gun Money of James II. A remarkably large collection, containing nearly
all the varieties. In condition from fair to about uncirculated; many are
very fine, the best a former owner could find out of hundreds examined.
Half Crowns. 1689: Jan., Mar., July, Aug., Sep., Dec. 1690: Apr., May
(large and small), July. 1690: King on horseback. Shillings. 1689:
Jan., Feb., Mar., July, Aug., Aug't, Sep'r, Sep't, 9, Oct, 10, Nov., Dec.
1690: Apr., May, may, June, Sep. Sixpences. 1689: Jan., Feb., June,
July, Aug., Sep'r, 7ber, Dec. 37 pieces. 25.00.
Java. ½ St. Fine. .35.
Java. 1 Stiver. Without date. Thick dump. Fine. .75.
Java. 1802. 2 Stubers. Oblong bar. Very good. 1.50.
Java. 1818. 2 Stubers. Oblong bar. Very good. 1.50.
Jamaica. Penny and Halfpenny. Alligator above shield. Nickel. Very good. .35.
Japan. Tempo. Oblong. (See cut.) Fine. .15.
Liberia. 1833. Negro, tree and ship. Uncirculated. Brown. .50.

Liberia.   1847.   Cent.   Palm tree.   Extremely fine.   .50.   Good.   .25.
Liberia.   1862.   Cent and Two Cents.   Fine.   .75.
Liberia.   1862.   Two Cents.   Proof.   1.25.   Extremely fine.   .50.
Monaco.   1838.   5, 10 Centimes.   Br. proof.   .50.
Malacca.   1250.   "Cock of the Walk" (See cut).   Very fine.   .35.
Meysore.   Elephant.   Thick dump.   5 Cash.   Very fine.   .50.
Meysore.   Lion.   Thick dump.   20 Cash.   Very fine.   .75.
Mexico.   Chihuahua.   1860.   Liberty seated.   ¼ R.   Very good.   .50.
Chihuahua.   1846.   ¼ R.   Indian.   Fine.   .60.   Very good.   .35.
Jalisco.   ¼, ⅛ R.   Female with flag.   Good.   1.00.
Sinaloa.   Head of Liberty.   ¼ R.   Fine.   .50.   Good.   .25.
Sonora.   Female with flag.   Cuartilla.   Very good.   .75.
Zacatecas.   Quartilla.   Temple and angel.   Almost uncirculated.   1.50.   Very good.
        1.00.
Zacatecas.   Octavo.   Temple and angel.   Very good.   1.00.
Guanaxuati.   1856.   Cuartilla.   Fine and rare.   1.00.
Mexico.   1864.   Centavo of Maxmilian.   Fine.   1.00.   Good.   .50.
Nicaragua.   1887.   2 Cents.   Br. proof.   .25.
Orange Free States.   1888.   Penny.   Brilliant proof.   .35.
Persia.   Fath Ali Schah.   1797-1834.   1½ Bisti.   Rabbit.   Very good.   1.00.
Same ruler.   1½ Bisti.   Sun-lion.   Fine.   1.00.
Portugal.   Maria II.   5 Reis.   Uncirculated.   Bright red.   .25.
Patagonia.   Orille–Antoine I.   1874.   2 Centavos.   Proof.   .25.
Portuguese Africa.   ½, 1 Macuta.   Very fine.   1 25.
Papal States.   Pius IX.   4 Soldi.   Bright.   .50.   Extra fine, olive.   .35.
Papal States.   Gregory XVI. and Pius IX.   Baiocco.   Uncirculated.   Bright.   .75.
Poland.   1831.   3 Grosze.   Uncirculated.   Brilliant red.   .25.
Roman Republic.   40, 4 Baiocchi.   Base silver.   Very fine and uncirculated.   1.50.
Roman Republic.   3 Baiocchi.   Uncirculated.   Bright red.   1.00.
Roumania.   5, 10 Bani.   Extremely fine.   .50.
Russia.   1775-1805.   5 Kopecs.   Weight, 2 oz.   Very fine.   .50.   Good.   .35.
Sierra Leone.   Prowling lion.   1791.   Cent.   Bronze proof.   1.00.
Sarawak.   Cent.   Bright.   1.00.   Fine.   .50.
Sandwich Islands.   Kamehameha III.   Hapi Haneri.   Uncirculated.   Bright red.
        .75.   Fine.   .50.
Siberia.   1764.   Set of 10, 5, 3, 2, 1, ½ Kopec, the latter (usually catalogued as ¼
        Kopec) very scarce.   All with Sable Foxes except the ½ Kopec.   Very
        fine.   7.50.
South Africa.   1890.   Penny.   Br. proof.   .25.
Suriname.   1764.   Coffee plant.   About uncirculated.   1.00.
Sweden.   Large Or.   Size 30.   1685.   Fine.   1.00.
States of Jersey.   1888.   1–12, 1–24 Sh.   Uncirculated.   Bright red.   .35.
Sicily.   1849.   Ferd. II.   ½, 1, 2 Tornese.   Uncirculated.   Bright red.   .75.
Sicily under Napoleon.   Head of Jerome Napoleon.   3 Grana.   Good.   .75.
Strasburg.   Siege Decime.   1814-1815.   L and N crowned.   Fine.   Pair.   .75.
St. Helena.   Halfpenny.   Very good.   .20.

War Medals.

United States.   Silver medal presented to John Bowen, by City of New York
        for the war with Mexico.   Arms of New York, rev., typical female point-
        ing to city and harbor—Cerro Gordo—Chapultepec—Cherubusco—Vera
        Cruz.   Very fine.   Size 32.   Weight 2 oz.   Av.   6.00.
Silver medal presented by South Carolina to Palmetto Regiment, Mexican War.
        Palmetto tree; rev., troops landing from boats.   Silver, ribbon attached.
        Very fine.   Size 31.   7.50.
"Death to traitors;" medal of the Iron Brigade, N. Y. Vol's; white metal, ribbon
        attached.   Good.   Size 24.   1.00.
West Virginia.   Liberty crowning a soldier, 1861-1865.   Copper.   Uncirculated.
        3.00.   Very good.   1.50.

Anhalt. Shield of arms crowned; rev., bear walking on wall. Order of "Albert the Bear," bronze proof. Size 20. 1.25.

England. Waterloo medal. Bust of Prince Regent; rev., Victory seated, "Wellington" above, "Waterloo, June 18, 1815" below. Silver, light scratches on obverse, ribbon attached. 5.00.

The following English medals all have head of Victoria on obverse and are silver of size 74 unless otherwise described.

"Ava." Rev., Victory seated; "To the Army of India, 1799–1826." Bar, "Ava," ribbon attached. Very fine. 5.00.

Army of Punjab. Rev., soldiers surrendering to mounted British officers. 1849. Two bars, "Mooltan and Goojerat," ribbon attached. Very fine. 6.00.

"Northwest Frontier." Rev., Victory crowning a naked warrior. Bar, "Northwest Frontier," ribbon attached. Very fine. 5.00.

"Pegu." Same reverse. Bar, "Pegu." Very fine. 3.50.

"Umbeyla." Same reverse. Bar, "Umbeyla." Very fine. 5.00.

Crimea. Four bars. "Alma, Balaklava, Inkermann, Sebastapol," ribbon attached. Very fine. 15.00.

Crimea. Rev., flying Victory placing wreath on warrior in Roman costume, "Crimea" in field. Three bars, "Sebastopol, Inkermann, Alma," ribbon attached. Very fine. 10.00.

Same. One bar, "Sebastopol," ribbon attached, very fine. 4.00. Another without bar but with swivel and ribbon, very fine. 3.00. Another, no bar or ribbon, very fine. 2.50.

India, 1857–58. Rev., Una and the lion. Bar, "Delhi," ribbon attached. Semi-proof. Rare. 6.00.

India, 1857–58. Same reverse. Bar, Lucknow. Very fine. 4.00.

India, 1857–58. Same reverse. Swivel and ribbon. Very fine. 3.00.

India, 1857–58. Same reverse. Bar, "Central India." Very fine. 4.00.

India, 1857–58. Same reverse. Two bars, "Lucknow," "Defense of Lucknow," ribbon attached. Fine. 6.00.

Baltic, 1854–55. Rev., Britannia seated, two fortresses in background. Bar and ribbon. Proof. 3.50.

China. Rev., trophy of arms, flags, etc., "China" below. Two bars, "Pekin 1860 and Taku Forts 1860," ribbon attached. Fine. 5.00.

South Africa. Rev., Lion and bush, "South Africa" above. Bar, "1879," ribbon attached. Very fine. 3.50.

Arctic Discoveries. Rev., Arctic scene, 1818–1855. Octagon; ribbon attached. Very fine. Size 22. Rare. 4.00.

1848. Rev., Victory crowning Wellington, "To the British Army, 1793–1814." Bar, "Badajoz," ribbon attached. Very fine. Rare. 6.00.

New Zealand. Head crowned, veil falling down behind; rev., wreath, "New Zealand Virtutis Honor." Ornamented bar and ribbon. Very fine. 4.00.

Abyssinia. Crowned and veiled head in centre of large star, between the points; "Abyssinia;" rev., name of wearer in wreath. Crown and ring with ribbon above. Semi-proof. Size 22. 5.00.

Veiled head of Victoria; rev., a number of semi-nude Ashantees fighting in bush with infantry. Bar and ribbon. Very fine. 3.50.

Egypt. Soudan. Bust of Queen; rev., sphinx. Bar, "El-teb-tamaai," ribbon attached. Fine proof. 6.00.

Egypt. Same design. Bar, "The Nile, 1884–85," ribbon attached. Fine proof. 6.00.

Egypt. Same design. Bar, "Suakim, 1885." Proof. 6.00.

Egypt. Same design. Bar, "Tel-el-kebir," ribbon attached. Fine proof. 6.00.

Bust of Queen; rev., sphinx, 1882, Egypt. Bar, "Tel-el-kebir," ribbon attached. Officers' medal. Semi-proof. Size 12. 3.00.

Afghanistan. Rev., elephant artillery. Bar "Ali Musjid," ribbon attached. Semi-proof. 6.00. Another, plain bar, with ribbon. Proof. 4.00.

Afghanistan. Same design. Bar, "Ahmed Khel," ribbon attached. Fine proof. 6.00.

Persia. Rev., Victory crowning Roman warrior. Bar, "Persia." Fine proof. 6.00.

Sutlej Campaign. Rev., Victory standing holding wreath, war trophies at her feet, Moodkee, 1845, below. Three bars, "Sobraon, Aliwal, Ferozeshuhur." Proof. 10.00.

Syria. 1848. Rev., Britannia seated on hippocampus. Bar, "Syria," ribbon attached. Brilliant proof. 6.00.

Coat of Arms; rev., "For long service and good conduct." Bar with ribbon. Proof. 4.00.

Star of five points, in centre sphinx and pyramids, "Egypt 1882." Rev., crowned monogram. Bar with star and crescent, ribbon attached. Given to English soldiers who served during the war against Arabi Pasha. Perfect. Bronze. Size 30. 3.50.

France. Napoleon III. Expedition to China, 1860. Head. Rev., names of battles. Ribbon with Chinese characters attached. Silver. Size 20. Unused. 3.50.

Same. Officers' size. With ribbon. Unused. Size 11. 2.50.

Same. Unused. Size 7. 1.50.

Napoleon III. For Mexican campaign. 1862–1863. Silver. Very fine. Ribbon attached. Size 20. 2.50.

Republic. Expedition to China, 1883–1885. Rev., names of battles. Silver. Size 20. Unused. 3.00.

Saxe-Gotha-Altenburg. The Altenburg rose; rev., ducal crown. Bronze. Very fine. Size 27. 1.00.

Turkey. For Crimea, 1855. Trophy of cannon, etc.; rev., cipher of Abdul Medjid. Silver. Size 24. Very fine. 2.00.

Numismatic Books and Pamphlets.

Steigerwalt's Illustrated History of United States and Colonial Coins. Many illustrations and the cheapest work of its class. Cloth. .75.

"Early Half Dimes," Harold P. Newlin, 1883. Full descriptions of the varieties of the early dates and also an interesting article on the whereabouts of all the known 1802 Half Dimes. Fine paper with broad margins. New. Edition very limited. Illustrated with plates. Cloth, 1.00. Paper (no plates) reduced to .25.

Madden's History of Jewish coinages. Many illustrations. 350 pages. Half morocco. New and uncut. 5.00.

Atlas Numismatique du Canada. Jos. Le Roux. 1883. 40 pages, with illustrations of all the 220 Canadian coins. Letter press in English and French. A valuable work. Paper covers. 1.00.

Silver coins of England. Henry. 1878. 48 pages. Illustrated pamphlet. .35.

Numisgraphics or a list of sale catalogues. Atinnelli, 1876. 134 pages. Paper covers. Rare. 2.00.

Haseltine's "Paper Money of the Colonies." Illustrated. Pamphlet. 5 plates. Reduced to .15.

Haseltine's "Confederate Notes and Bonds." .25.

"Das Romische Ass." German. 24 pages. 6 plates. .35.

The Naturalist's Directory. Cassino. 1886. 4801 names. 1.00.

Coins, medals and seals. W. C. Prime. 114 plates. 292 pages. Cloth. New York, 1861. 3.50.

Coins of the Grand Master of Malta. R. Morris, Boston, 1884. 6 plates. 70 pages Cloth. 1.50.

Le Medaillier Du Canada. Jos. LeRoux, Montreal. 1888. Cloth with additional paper supplement. Illustrates over 1800 Canadian coins and medals. 6.00.

Historia Numorum. A Manual of Greek Numismatics by Barclay V. Head, Assistant Keeper of the Department of Coins and Medals in the British Museum. 1887. Hundreds of illustrations. 818 pages. Half morocco. By far the best work of its class ever issued. 12.50.

New Varieties of Gold and Silver Coins, etc. Eckfeldt and Dubois. Phila., 1850. Covers loose. Illustrated. Contains about 50 to 75 cts. worth of real gold fastened to page 45 illustrating metals. 1.50.

"Early Coins of America," by S. S. Crosby. 331 pages. 12 heliotype plates and 110 fine cuts, large quarto. In parts as originally issued. 6.00.

Marvin's Masonic Medals. 17 plates. Also, accurate descriptions of 744 medals. Heavy paper. The standard American publication. 350 pages. New. 10.00.

Curiosities.

Knight of Pythias sword. Handsome steel scabbard and mountings. Knights, Pilgrims, Eagles, etc. Very fine and desirable. Probably made for an officer and cost about $30. Uninjured by use. In buckskin cover. 10.00.

A single hair from the head of Henry Clay. Taken when the body was lying in state at Baltimore. .50.

Massive brown agate paper weight, in shape of a seal and handle, cut from one piece. Very handsome and valuable. 5¾ inches long, 2¾ inches wide at top. 5.00.

Seal. Similar. Red agate. 2⅛ inches long. Handsome. 2.50.

Marble paper weight. "Appian Way," near Ravenna, Italy. .75.

Egyptian scarabeus. Very fine. 1.50.

Olive wood pipe. Liberty bell design. New. .50.

Japan. Native painted photo. on glass in case. Very odd. 1.00.

Japan. Opium pipe. New. .75.

Piece of gold ore, oval, polished ready for mounting as a breast pin. Size 26. 5.00.

Aztec Idol, carved from pumice stone, prehistoric, very fine specimen, dug from mound near Durango, Mexico. 15x9x7 inches. Very desirable. 100.00.

Hindoo Idol. Fine white marble. Old. 16 x 9½ in. 25.00.

Old Japanese. God of Plenty. Very odd. Bronze. 6 x 4 in. 10.00.

Old Japanese. Dog Foy on stump. Bronze. 4 x 4 in. 10.00.

Agate egg. Full size of a hen's egg. Very handsome. 1.50.

Paper weight. Glass. View of foreign building. 3 inches. .50.

Ostrich egg. South Africa. Fine large specimen. 2.50.

Indian doe-skin slipper. Fancy bead work. Very fine. 1.00.

Pottery vase and ball stopper from Cyprus. Old and valuable. 2.00.

Ivory queen, black, elaborately carved dress. 3.00.

Ancient bronze statuette. Venus. 2½ in. From Syria. 3.00.

Ancient bronze statuette. Curious animal. 1½ in. From Syria. 2.00.

Ancient Roman spearhead, iron, 3½ in. From German Mound. 2.00.

Terra Vert Ancient Egyptian ornaments, Lion, Anubias, etc. 5 pcs. Lot for 7.50.

Plumes of the Egret or White Crane, snow white, 22 in., Florida. 2.00.

Skin of Mottled Crane, very fine, 27 in., Florida. 1.50.

Curious polished stone, natural scene resembling a river and bank with trees and foliage. 10½ in. 5.00.

Remarkable clay idol from Guatemala. Human figure with tail. Head broken from body (has been mended), and part of legs missing. Curious and rare. 2.50.

Florida sea-beans. 14 pcs. .75.

Gourd Dish. From Peruvian mound. Fine. 1.00.

Brazil. Nut-case filled with nuts. 4x4. 2.00.

Curious bark writing in native India characters, 3 fine specimens, and a piece of tappa cloth. 4 pcs. 1.00.

Pair of very old galoshes. 1.50.

Handsome polished tiger-eye ball, suitable for cane or umbrella handle. 1¾ in. in diameter. 1.00.

Remarkable old mortar and pestle. The mortar is dated 1694, and has odd dragon head handles. 10.00.

Pair of handles from very old desk, ram's head with ring in mouth. Bronze. 1.00.

Apache horn spoon. 9 in. in length. 4 in. wide. 1.50.

Wooden vases. 5½ in. high. Made from the Great Elm on Boston Common. 2 pcs. 1.00.

Geode, Ill. 4½ in. wide, 2 in. high. Nice specimen. 1.50.

Amethyst crystals. Hungary. 4x3½ in. 1.50.

Peacock Brass Incense Burner. 14 in. high. Beautifully carved with Persian
    figures. A rare Persian ornament. 15.00.

Bowl. Brass. Persia. A beautiful, rare and valuable specimen. 10 in. in diame-
    ter, 6 in. deep. The sides beautifully ornamented with procession of 12
    odd figures of priests and animals. 10.00.

Mounted lens (2), each 2 in., on stand. 1.00.

Olive wood seal top. .25.

Brass spoon mould. Very old. 7¾ in. 2.00.

Fine specimen of opal in matrix. Mexico. 1.50.

Gold ore, oval polished specimens, once set in sleeve-buttons, contain considerable
    gold. Size 9. 4 pcs. 5.00.

Curious match-safe, form of beetle. 4 in. .50.

Brass candlesticks. Assortment of designs, all polished. 43 pcs. 15.00.

Brass candlestick, snuffers and tray, polished. Old and desirable. 3.50.

Very old paper-snapper, brass dragon. 5 in. 1.00.

Bone spoons, very old, 6 inches. 4 pcs. 1.50.

Bone two-pronged fork, very old. 6½ in. 1.00.

Very old powder-flask. 2.00.

Very old knife, four broad blades, three with crescent projections to cut button-holes,
    handle about 1½ inch at bottom and only ½ inch at top. Curious. 2.50.

Very old wooden spoon, large bowl, elaborately carved handle; evidently a high-
    priced soup-spoon. 9 in. 1.50.

Beautiful necklace of 50 handsome large Brazilian agate beads, finely matched in
    size and markings. 5.00.

Patrick Henry. A very fine bust of bronzed zinc. 14 inches high. 5.00.

Curious carved ivory clenched hands (tops of old seals). 4 pcs. 2.00.

South Sea Islander's wooden spear. In two pieces (made that way). 32 inches.
    1.50.

Small figure of Napoleon, lead. very old. .50.

Ivory chessmen from Siam. Old. 3 pcs. 1.50.

Egypt. Goddess of Evil, Taur. 3500 years old. Hyena-headed goddess with big
    feet. Fine. 2¾ inches. Very rare. 10.00.

Antique lamp, Roman, of the kind used in Biblical times. Very fine specimen.
    5.00.

Paper cutter. Brass. India. Double god at end. 9½ inches. 2.50.

Whale's tooth. Polished specimen. 6¾ in. 2.00.

Hammer. Walrus tusk head. 1.00.

Marline spike. Walrus tusk. 12 in. 1.50.

Collection of Proof Sets.

1859-1891. A collection of 34 Proof Sets, inclusive of both sets of 1873 ("Old"
    and " New" style) in choice condition. Cheap at 150.00.

Collection of War Cards and Tokens.

A splendid collection of War Cards and Tokens formed by the former owner at the
    period and struck to his order. The collection (so marked) contains 24
    silver, 470 nickel and about 500 copper—all different (about 1000)—and
    there are over 300 in addition (100 nickel) that may be part of the collec-
    tion, but have not had time to compare to ascertain. The silver cards are
    rare, and the large collection of nickel cards, *all brilliant proofs*, could not
    be equalled; the copper cards and tokens are also proofs or uncirculated.
    A valuable collection. 1335 pcs. 50.00.

Historic China.

All dark blue unless otherwise described.

Orders for Historic China must be absolute sale, with risk of breakage taken by purchaser. Owing to trouble and expense of packing carefully, they cannot be sent on approval.

Washington Masonic Plate. View of Mount Vernon in centre. Justice blindfolded and wearing Masonic apron holds oval picture of Washington. Kneeling figure of Liberty with pole surmounted by cap inscribed "Liberty." Below, "America and Independence." On border circle of 15 States, including Vermont and Kentucky—first two admitted. Breakfast plate. 15.00.

Landing of Lafayette at Castle Garden, 1824. Ships, cannon, soldiers, view of Castle Garden, etc. Dinner plate. 10.00.

Same. Dessert plate. 5.00.

Commodore MacDonnough's Victory on Lake Erie. View of Naval Engagement. Dinner plate. 10.00.

Same. Dessert plate. A little worn. 3.00.

Fairmount, near Philadelphia. Dinner plate. 4.00.

Same. Large soup dish. 4.00.

Upper Ferry Bridge over River Schuylkill. Dinner plate. 4.00.

Water-works, Philadelphia (at Broad and Market, where public buildings now stand). Breakfast plate. Black. 3.00.

Near Fishkill, Hudson River. Dinner plate. Brown. 4.00.

East View of La Grange, Residence of Marquis Lafayette. Dinner plate. 5.00.

Trenton Falls. Breakfast plate. 3.00.

College at Richmond, Va. Breakfast plate. Light blue. 2.00.

The Residence of the late Richard Jordan, New Jersey (country scene with farm house and barn, cow and little fat Quaker in broad-rim hat. Jordan was a maker of plates). Breakfast. Pink. 3.00.

City Hall, New York. Deep saucer. 2.00.

The following are mended, but in fairly desirable condition.

MacDonnough's Victory. Dinner plate. 4.00.

Same. Breakfast plate. 2.50.

Library. Philadelphia. Breakfast plate. 2.00.

Baker's Falls, Hudson River. Dinner plate. Black. 1.50.

Pitchers. A pair. Each with old-fashioned eagle holding scroll in mouth inscribed "E Pluribus Unum." These are slightly mended at bottom, but so skillfully as to be scarcely perceptible. Pair 10.00.

Old-Fashioned Porcelain Tiles. Woman with big hoops, man rolling barrel. etc. All different. 6 pcs. 6.00.

Porcelain Cup and Saucer. Royal Sevres. From the set of King Louis Philippe of France at the Chateau Fontainebleau. Marked with the king's monogram and name of chateau. Very desirable. 25.00.

Diamonds, Jewelry, etc.

The owner of the following lot of diamonds, jewelry, etc., has placed it in my hands to sell at rates which are about one-half cost to him, and from 10 per cent. to 25 per cent. below lowest *wholesale* rates. They could not be bought from retailers for less than they cost the owner.

Gold Ring. Three white perfect diamonds, about one carat each, neatly mounted. Cost 225.00. 140.00.

Gold Ring. Fine white diamond, over one carat. A pretty little sparkler. Cost 85.00. 50.00.

Gold Ring. Fine white diamond of about ¾ carat weight. Cost 60.00. 40.00.

Handsome moon-stone pin, the stone finely carved with a moon-face. Surrounded by four pretty little diamonds, size usually selling at 10 to 15 dollars each, retail. Finely mounted with gold setting and pin. 37.50.

Diamond pin. The centre stone is about one carat, eight diamonds surrounding it. All are guaranteed genuine diamonds, but of the poorer quality, almost black and irregularly cut. Only good as samples. 10.00.

Antique Gold Beads. Large string. Weight in gold about ½ oz. Troy. 10.00.

Pair of Antique Gold Ear-rings. Pendant form. 5.00.

Pair of Antique Gold Ear-rings. Hoop form. 5.00.

Pair of Antique Gold Ear-rings. Oval. 5.00.

Antique Silver Cream Pitcher and Sugar Bowl. Sterling silver. Have not had weighed accurately, but from scales tried on they weighed about 35 oz. Troy. 60.00.

Gold Watch. About 100 years old. Running order. Fine antique face. 15.00.

Silver Bull-Eye Watch. Antique. 5.00.

Gold Bracelet. Form of a snake. Two diamonds for eyes. 20.00.

Sleeve Buttons. Pair of curious Japanese. Pair of quails, flowers, etc., on each in gold on rubber. 7.50.

Large Oval Medallion or Breast-pin. Cupid and dove painted on porcelain and mounted in handsome gold frame. The painting is superb, and pronounced by several artists to whom it was shown as elegant work. Cost 50.00. 30.00.

Mary, Queen of Scots. Exquisite little painting on porcelain. 5.00.

Gold Padlock and Key. Suitable for watch-chain or bracelet. 3.50.

Handsome string of 33 pretty "cat-eyes." 7.50.

Madonna and Child. Medallion or breast-pin. Beautifully painted and in magnificent carved ivory frame. 10.00.

Raphael's Madonna and Child and the well-known Cherubs. Painted on porcelain in gold frames. Breast-pin and ear-rings (the cherubs are the ear-rings). Set 12.50.

Napoleon the Great. Pretty miniature on porcelain in gold frame. Old. 10.00.

Mosaic. Oval. St. Peter's at Rome. Very pretty. 5.00.

Antique Watch Key. Bead work. Very old. 2.50.

Antique Watch-Key. Equally old. Large oval stone in centre. 2.00.

Bracelet. 6 oval female heads finely carved out of as many different shades of lava. 2.50.

Byzantine Madonna. Very old. The crown on heads of Mary and child Jesus, as well as a very elaborate frame work surrounding, is made of the finest possible silk filigree work interspersed with stones (some may be gems), including some genuine pearls. 75.00.

Carvings. Ivory. Japanese Priest and Attendant. Beautiful work. 25.00.

Ivory. The Dance of Death. An unique and very old and curious piece of Japanese carving. 50.00.

Ivory. Japanese Figure on Horseback. Very intricate and exquisite piece of carving. 35.00.

Japanese Stone Carving. The Philosopher. Handsome. 12.50.

Bamboo Carving. Lion and cub resting under a tree. Extraordinary piece. 10.00.

Ebony Carving from Brazil. An exquisite piece representing Venus and her dove. 25.00.

Antique Bronzes. Bronze lamp from the ruins of Pompeii. 20.00.

Pompeain Bronze. Fox. 15.00.

Pompeain Bronze. The Gladiator. 15.00.

Roman Bronze. Athlete. 10.00.

Japanese Bronze. Curious piece. 5.00.

Japanese Bronze. Angry Dragon. Very elaborate and magnificent specimen. 15.00.

Cloisonne Enamel Incense Burner. Parrot with removable wings. Enameled in colors on copper. Choice piece. 10.00.

Antique Furniture. Very old Norwegian Cabinet. With beautifully carved panels, supported by richly carved columns, dated 1719. 85.00.

Very old Norwegian Church Chest. With two handsomely carved panels, repre-

senting the Adoration and the Presentation in the Temple, with ara-
besque design on side, surmounted on open base. Very remarkable
piece, dated 1640. 125.00.

Numismatic Books.

Conder. "An Arrangement of Provincial Coins, Tokens, etc.," by James Conder. Ipswich, 1798. 12mo, 330 pp., 3 plates, half morocco, clean.
The standard authority on its series. 12.50.

American Bond Detector. 100 pp., 21 plates of fac-similes of U. S. Bonds, etc.,
9 plates of U. S. and foreign coins in metallic colors. Long folio, cloth.
Issued by U. S. Treas. Dept., 1869. Rare and very desirable. 10.00.

Heath. Counterfeit Detector. Boston, 1867. Folio, 39 pp. 11 plates and
loose duplicates. 5.00.

Philips. The Paper Currency of the American Colonies. Roxbury, published
by W. Elliott Woodward, 1865. Small 4to, 264 pp., unbound. 2 vols.
Scarce. 5.00.

Satterlee. Presidential Medals and Tokens. New York, 1862. 8vo, 84 pp.,
cloth. Loose photo. of author. Scarce. 2.50. Same, paper cover. 2.00.

Bolen's Medals. Cards and Fac-similes, an accurate Catalogue of, by E. L. Johnson. 8vo, cloth. Springfield, 1882. 1.00.

Bowring, J. The Decimal System in Numbers, Coins and Accounts. 120 engravings of coins. 8vo. London. 1854. 2.00.

Descriptive Catalogue of the Seavey Collection. Bought by Loring G. Parmelee.
8 plates of photographs. 8vo, half morocco. Privately printed. 4.00.

Coins of the World. 12 fac-simile plates. 12mo. In paper cover. Philadelphia. 1849. 1.00.

Coin Book. With 16 plates of figures. 8vo. Philadelphia, 1872. 2.00.

Du Bois, W. E. Brief Account of the U. S. Mint Collection. Plate. Small
12mo, half roan. Rare. Philadelphia, 1846. 2.00.

Eckfeldt and Du Bois. A Manual of Gold and Silver Coins of all Nations, struck
within the past century. With engravings. 4to, cloth. Philadelphia,
1842. 2.50.

New Varieties of Gold and Silver Coins, Counterfeits, and Bullion. Second
edition. 8vo. New York, 1851. .50.

Ede, J. A View of the Gold and Silver Coins of all Nations. Exhibited in
above 400 copper-plate cuts. With descriptions. Square 12mo, calf.
London. 2.00.

Evans, G. G. Illustrated History of the United States Mint, with a complete
description of American Coinage. Illustrated with phototypes, steel-
plate portraits and wood-cuts, etc. New and revised edition. 8vo,
half morocco. Philadelphia, 1885. 1.50.

Hagen, J. G. F. Verzeichniss eines Zahlreichen Original Munzcabinets. Front-
ispiece. 12mo, half vellum. Nurnberg. 1769. 1.00.

Hawkins, Ed. The Silver Coins of England arranged and described, with re-
marks on British Money previous to the Saxon Dynasties. 47 plates.
8vo, half roan. London, 1841. 4.00.

Haym, N. F. Thesauri Britannici pars altera, seu Museum Nummarium com-
plexum Numos Graecos et Latinos omnis metalli. 51 plates of coins.
4to, old calf. 1765. 3.00.

Henry, J. The Series of English Coins in Copper, Tin and Bronze. Small 4to.
London, 1879. 1.00.

Hofmann, L. W. Alter und Neuer Muntz-Schlussel. 93 plates of figures.
Small 4to, half vellum. Nurnberg, 1683. 3.00.

Humphreys, H. N. The Coinage of the British Empire. Illustrated by fac-
similes of the coins of each period, worked in gold, silver and copper.
8vo. London, 1855. 4.00.

Joachim, J. F. Sammlung von Deutschen Münzen. 25 folded plates. 12mo,
boards. Leipzig, 1755. 1.50.

Klotz, C. A. Historia Numorum Contumeliosorum et Satyricorum cum figuris. 16mo, boards. 1765. 1.00.

Loubat, J. F. The Medallic History of the United States of America, 1776-1876. With 170 etchings by Jules Jacquemart. 2 vols., 4to, uncut. New York: Published by the author, 1878. 25.00.

Manual of Roman Coins. With 21 plates. 8vo. London, 1865. 2.50.

Mason's Coin and Stamp Collector's Magazine, 1867-72. Vols. 1 to 5, and Nos. 1 to 6 of Vol. 6, in Nos. All published. Lot 3.00.

Introduction a la Connoissance des Médailles, par C. Patin. 16mo, vellum, sheep. Paris, 1667. .75.

Seguin, P. Selecta Numismata Antiqua. With cuts. 4to, sheep. Paris, 1666. 1.25.

Simon, J. An Essay towards an Historical Account of Irish Coins, etc. 4to, half calf. Dublin, 1749. 4.00.

Streinnius, R. De Gentibus et Familiis Romanorum. Small 4to, boards. Venetiis, 1571. 1.50.

Tristan, I. Commentaires Historiques—les Vies, eloges et censures des Empereurs, Imperatrices, Cæsars et Tyrans de l'Empire Romain, le tout illustré de l'exacte explication des revers enigmatiques de plusieurs centaines de médailles, etc. Many fine copper-plates. Folio, old calf. Paris, 1635. 3.50.

Wharton, J. Memorandum concerning Small Money and Nickel Alloy Coinage. With illustrations. Pamphlet. .75.

Another. Second Edition. 1.00.

Woodward, W. Elliot. A List of Washington Memorial Medals. Two fine portraits. 8vo, half morocco. Only 50 copies printed. 1865. 5.00.

Snelling, T. The Doctrine of Gold and Silver Computations. With tables and copper-plates. 8vo, half roan. London, 1766. 1.00.

Early Spanish and Portuguese Coinage in America. J. Carson Brevoort. Privately printed. 4to, 5 plates. Boston, 1885. 1.50.

The Coinage of Morelos (Mexico). Illustrated. 4to. Lyman Low. Privately printed. 1886. .75.

History of the Bills of Credit or Paper Money issued by New York. John H. Hickcox. 103 pages. Large paper, uncut. Albany, 1866. 3.50.

The Currency of the Confederate States of America, by Raphael Thian. Washington, 1885. 2.50.

Varieties of the Copper Issues of the United States Mint in the year 1794. Edward Maris, M. D. Philadelphia, 1869. 2.00.

Assignats and Mandats. Stephen D. Dillaye. Philadelphia, 1877. .75.

Addison's Dialogues on Medals. 8 plates. 1.00.

Medals by Giovanni Cavino (the Paduan). Richard H. Lawrence. Illustrated. Privately printed. New York, 1883. 1.25.

American Journal of Numismatics. 1866-1888. Vol.'s 1 to 22 complete, Vol. 23, Nos. 1, 2, 3. The first 8 Vol.'s bound in two books, one half, the other full morocco. Excepting the last few issues, easily procured, a complete set of this valuable journal, replete with numismatic information. 35.00.

The Coin Collector's Manual. H. Noel Humphreys. Over 150 illustrations on wood and steel. 726 pages. Half morocco. London, 1871. 6.00.

Medals Awarded by Foreign Societies to Kane, Hayes and Hall. Prof. J. E. Nourse, U. S. N. 1 plate. Cloth. 1876. Rare. 1.25.

The Copper, Tin and Bronze Coinage and Patterns for Coins of England. H. Montagu. Many illustrations. Thick paper. Uncut. 3.00.

Catalogue of Parmelee sale. Unpriced. .50.

Another. Priced and bound in cloth. 1.50.

Catalogue of Robt. C. Davis Collection. Priced and bound in cloth. 1.50.

Catalogue of the Thomas Warner Collection, 1884. Finely bound in boards. Large paper. Printed prices. 1.25.

Descriptive Catalogue of a Cabinet of Roman Family Coins, belonging to the Duke of Northumberland, by Rear-Admiral William Henry Smith. Large 4to. Cloth. 323 pages. Privately printed. London, 1856. 7.50.

Confederate, Colonial Notes, etc.

Confederate. 1861. $1,000. Montgomery. A beautiful note, nearly uncirculated. Cancelled by small L L cut, which has been mended so as to scarcely show. 50.00.

1861. $500. Montgomery. Extremely fine. Perfectly uncancelled. One of the best $500 notes known. In this condition, exceedingly rare. 65.00.

The following C. S. A. notes are cancelled with clean x x cuts, nothing missing from note, and could be easily mended so as to make cancellation imperceptible.

1861. Sept. 2. $50. Train of cars. Very fine. 2.00.
1861. Sept. 2. $20. Female and globe. Very fine. 1.50.
1861. Sept. 2. $10. Group of Indians. Fine. 1.50.
1861. Sept. 2. $10. Wagon loaded with cotton bales. Very fine. Scarce. 2.00.
1861. Sept. 2. $5. Group of females. Practically uncirculated. 2.00.
1861. Sept. 2. $5. Group of females. Letters A, B and C. 3 pc. Uncancelled. Very good. Lot 5.00.
1861. Sept. 2. $5. Group of females. Letter A. Uncancelled. Very good. 2.00.
Confederate Note Album. Bechtel's. With 42 notes, nearly all uncirculated, and some very scarce, mounted in proper spaces in the album. 8.50.
C. S. A. $100 Bond. Act of Feb. 28, 1861. Haseltine No. 5. A little stained. .75.
Continental. $20. May 10, 1775. The rare long note with colored end. Very fine. 7.50.
Colonial. Mass. 1776. 4 sh. Codfish and Pine Tree. Fine. 2.50.
Mass. 1778. 6 pence. Codfish and Pine Tree. Very fine. 3.00.
Mass. 1780. $1, 2. 3, 4, 5, 7, 8. Very fine. Cancelled. Payment secured by United States and bearing devices similar to same values 1779 issue of Continental money. Lot 2.00.
New York. 1776. Aug. 13. $5. Candelabra. Good. 1.00.
New York. 1776. Aug. 13. $10. Elephant. Good. 1.00.
New Jersey. 1756. 1, 3, 12 sh. Uncir'd. .75.
New Jersey. 1776. 18 d, 3 sh. Uncir'd. .50.
Penn'a. 1764. 3 pence. *Printed by Ben. Franklin.* Uncir'd. .50.
Penn'a. 1764. June 18. 20 sh. *Printed by Ben. Franklin.* Good. Scarce. 1.00.
South Carolina. 1779. $90. Large note. Hercules and lion. Very fine. 1.00.
Broken Bank Bills. Good to uncirculated. All different. 17 pcs. 1.50.
Chihuahua. 1878. 25 Cent. Girl and sheep. Very fine. .50.
Hungarian Fund. $1. Louis Kossuth. 1852. Fine. 1.00.
Card Checks. War necessity money. 5, 25, 75 cts., J. M. Christy. 2 cts., J. S. Swartley, Greenville. 1 cent, Sandlake. Rare lot. 1.50.
Connecticut Lottery Ticket. For benefit of the College of New Jersey. 1753. 1.00.
Paterson, N. J., Lottery Ticket. Old. 1.00.
Massachusetts Semi-Annual State Lottery Ticket. According to act of March 2, 1790. 1.00.

www.ingramcontent.com/pod-product-compliance
Lightning Source LLC
Chambersburg PA
CBHW022154020726
47496CB00008B/2705